poppy

ROSIE RUSHTON

D0802704

SCHOLASTIC INC.

New York Toronto London Auckland Sydney
Mexico City New Delhi Hong Kong

ISBN 0-439-28664-6

Copyright © 1996 by Rosie Rushton. All rights reserved.
Published by Scholastic Inc., 555 Broadway, New York, NY 10012,
by arrangement with Hyperion Books for Children, an imprint of Buena
Vista Books, Inc. SCHOLASTIC and associated logos are trademarks
and/or registered trademarks of Scholastic Inc.

12 11 10 9 8 7 6 5 4 3 2 1   1 2 3 4 5 6/0

Printed in the U.S.A.   01

First Scholastic printing, March 2001

contents

poppy

presenting poppy

Poppy Field had parents who adored her, an elder sister who rarely teased her, a large house with Corinthian pillars on either side of the front door, and the sort of figure that high-fibre breakfast cereal manufacturers use in their adverts. She got her copper-coloured hair and mahogany eyes from her father, and her olive skin and total inability to sing in tune from her mother. She was rarely miserable, largely because, in all her thirteen years and eight months, the only real inconveniences that life had thrown in her path were the death of four goldfish in rapid succession and her total inability to grasp the basic principles of physics and chemistry. The latter didn't worry her, since she had already decided to become the country's youngest agony aunt upon leaving school, and a knowlege of magnetic fields wouldn't really help her.

Possibly because she had so few of her own, other people's problems had always been a matter of deep concern to Poppy. She believed that everyone had the right to be as happy as she was, and when she saw they were not, she felt compelled to do something about it. This preoccupation kept her very busy. It was Poppy who organised Year Nine's sponsored line dance for Comic Relief, Poppy who wrote impassioned pieces in the school magazine on every topic from parcels for Romania to the need for ramps at the public library, and Poppy to whom everyone turned at the first sign of a crisis. Her total absorption with their problems, combined with an unshakeable certainty that she could put everything right, was enormously comforting to those grappling with the inflated expectations of their teachers, the unreasonable behaviour of their parents or, as in the case of her very best friend, Livi, the disappearance of their boyfriend into the arms of Mia Fazackerly, who had legs up to her armpits and a year round *Baywatch* tan.

Poppy was not a goody-goody in any sense of the word, but she could see no point in being difficult for the sake of it. Hence, she broke only those rules she thought unfair or stupid in the first place, and having made her point, set about getting them changed. This crusading zeal made her enormously popular with her peers but rather less so with her teachers. Mrs. Joll, who had Poppy for PSE lessons, once remarked that the initials should really stand not for Personal and Social Education but for Poppy Sorts Everything.

It has to be said that since she viewed the emotional traumas of her friends as far more deserving of her time than schoolwork could ever be, Poppy's school grades hurtled up and down in direct relation to the number of problems she was attempting to solve at the time.

None of these problems was related to her own home life, which ran on smoothly oiled wheels as it always had. Poppy's father, Leo Field, was a tall elegant man who ran his own company, selling gazebos and stone goddesses and reproduction Japanese bird baths. When he was not persuading the well-heeled to part with cash, he played off a three handicap at the Waterline Golf and Country Club and was a leading light in the Abingvale Photographic Society, where his *Mist on a May Morning* had won him Black and White Photograph of the Year.

Her mother, Celia, divided her time between giving intimate ladies' lunch parties and playing for the Waterline ladies' tennis team. She didn't work, pointing out to her more career-minded friends that creating the right home environment and raising a family was a full-time job in itself, and besides, Leo made enough money for all their needs. She gave Poppy none of the problems her friends seemed to endure with their mothers; if Poppy wanted new clothes, she simply charged them to one of her mother's many store accounts; when she organised sleepovers, her mother produced vast quantities of pepperoni pizza and home-made blueberry ice cream and rarely said anything about keeping the noise down.

Melissa, her almost-eighteen-year-old sister, was also a highly accommodating sibling, perfectly prepared to lend Poppy silk shirts, bronze blusher, unladdered tights, and use of her hot brush. She would also skim through Poppy's math homework with all the ease expected of one who had Cambridge University positively pleading for her presence. She was going to have a Gap year first, travelling to Australia, courtesy of the air ticket she had persuaded her parents to give her as an eighteenth-birthday present. She didn't look at all like Poppy, having blue eyes, porcelain-white skin, and bobbed hair the colour of ripened corn, but she shared Poppy's belief that you could achieve anything you wanted if you simply employed the right tactics. And if Melissa was more concerned in achieving her own ends, while her sister wanted to make the entire world happy, they both pursued their aims so charmingly that old ladies in church called them "those lovely Field girls" and bemoaned the fact that there weren't more like them.

The only member of Poppy's family who could be thought to present her with anything like a problem was Granny Jay. Poppy adored Granny Jay from the bottom of her heart, and there were those who said that it was from this maternal grandparent that Poppy had inherited her stubborn nature and refusal to take no for an answer. Granny Jay was four feet eleven, shaped like a cottage loaf, with blue-rinsed hair, an iron will, and a tendency to talk in proverbs. She had lived, much to the consternation of Poppy's mother, in the same small Victorian terraced cottage beside the Leehampton canal for the past fifty-one years and resisted all attempts on the part of her solicitous family to get her to move somewhere more suitable for a lady of her advancing years. "A tree transplanted bears no fruit," she would assert forcefully, adding that she wasn't going anywhere till they carried her out feet first.

The problem of "what to do with Granny Jay" was one which had taken up much of her parents' time and conversation over the past few months, but this morning, when she was supposed to be working out the speed at which a train going from Edinburgh to London would pass the one going from London to Glasgow—as if anybody cared—Poppy had hit upon the perfect solution.

Tonight she would present the family with her idea, which she was quite sure would be acclaimed as little short of brilliant. But in the meantime, she had a more immediate and taxing problem to deal with.

Of all the challenges which Poppy Field willingly undertook, sorting out Livi Hunter's love life was proving the hardest of all.

poppy does some propping up

This latest crisis in the love life of her best friend had started at precisely ten fifteen that morning, when, between the end of French and the beginning of chemistry, Ben Bryant, with whom Livi had been agonisingly in love for three weeks and two days, had told her she lacked the sophistication necessary for an ongoing liaison with him and that he was attaching himself to Mia Fazackerly, who wore Paloma Picasso perfume to school and had made smouldering gazes into an art form. This rejection was all the more poignant because it was only two days since Valentine's Day, when Livi had spent a week's allowance on an outsize chocolate heart and a little red Cupid with a white plastic bow and arrow as symbols of her undying devotion. Ben had given her a card, which had been a source of great joy to her until she discovered that eight other girls in her year had received identical copies.

Despite firm instructions from Poppy that she was not to give Ben, whose ego was already inflated enough, the satisfaction of seeing her upset, Livi had dissolved into a small crumpled heap, declared that her life was as good as over, and proceeded to lock herself in the loo for the duration of chemistry. She had made Poppy promise, not only to tell the Horrific Horage that she had a migraine, but also not to breathe a word to a single soul about what had happened. Quite how this latest development was to be kept secret when Ben and Mia were wrapped round one another like hamsters on a cold morning, Poppy was not quite sure, but if Livi wanted her silence, that was what she would have.

Poppy had set herself the target of consoling Livi by the end of lunch break. She had eight minutes to go, and as yet her success was not very apparent.

"Come on, Livi, do cheer up—it's not the end of the world!" she said encouragingly, removing a soggy tissue from her friend's hand and replacing it with a dry one. Livi sniffed.

"What's wrong with her?" whispered Hayley Spicer, dumping her lunch box on the bench and eyeing Livi quizzically.

"Oh, it's nothing, she'll be fine," said Poppy. "Just life and stuff—you know."

"Oh," said Hayley, who clearly didn't.

Livi tugged miserably at a wayward strand of blond hair. Having had her shoulder-length locks cut short a month before, she now wished she hadn't and kept pulling at two-inch-long strands in the hope of somehow extending them.

Her pale violet eyes filled up once more with tears.

"I can't face geography," she said. "You'll have to go on without me."

Poppy sighed. This was getting ridiculous.

"Livi, you can't keep dodging lessons just because Ben or Mia are in the same set," she protested.

"Watch me," snapped Livi.

Poppy found it quite amazing that anyone's distress over a boy could take such dramatic proportions. Livi had spent the previous hour weeping into her cheese and pickle sandwich, declaring that if only her thighs were smaller and her boobs bigger, and if her face wasn't so fat and her mother would fork out for some decent gear, Ben would have stayed with her, she knew he would. Poppy, whose opinion of Ben was on a par with her view of amoebic dysentery, had said that she reckoned Livi was well shot of him, whereupon Livi had howled even more and said the trouble with Poppy was that she just didn't understand about matters of the heart.

Hunting in her locker for *Mountains and Valleys of Western Europe* with one hand while patting Livi on the shoulder with the other, Poppy reflected that there was some truth in that. Livi was her best friend and she loved her dearly, but she couldn't see why she got herself into such a state over boys. Poppy had nothing against the male species as such—she just couldn't imagine going all weak-kneed and pathetic over any of them. Livi seemed to think that unless you were half a couple you had somehow failed as a member of the human race, whereas Poppy had better things to do with her time than worry about whether some guy was going to phone her—and she was perfectly sure that she would never go into a decline if they didn't.

Not that she had actually had to put that philosophy to the test, since a large proportion of the boys in her year were falling over themselves to take her out and her only problem was that by Wednesday of each week she had to make a decision as to which one she would favour with her attentions the coming weekend. And if whichever hunky guy she chose took it upon himself to assume that two hours of Rollerblading in her company meant he had an exclusive claim on her attentions for the ensuing term, that was his problem. Poppy prided herself on having life well and truly sussed.

"What is wrong, Livi?" persisted Hayley, swinging her school bag over her shoulder. "Is it because Ben's chucked you?"

Livi shot her a horrified glance.

"How did you know?" she hissed.

Get real, thought Poppy. Hayley Spicer was to school gossip what radar was to the British fighting forces. She was also very outspoken; she never meant to be tactless, but sometimes Poppy wished she would just keep quiet.

"Oh, everyone knows," said Hayley airily. "Mia says he's been going off you for ages—pity you didn't dump him first, really."

Fat chance of that, thought Poppy. Livi hung on to her boyfriends like a limpet on a rock, and when they did drop her, she spent days chastising herself for everything from her lack of kissing technique to the fact that her two front teeth were uneven. Livi did not have a very high opinion of herself.

It was just as well, considered Poppy, that she was always on hand to pick up the pieces, because Livi was not only totally inept at handling boys, but completely useless in any sort of crisis.

"Come on, forget Ben," she said, pulling a reluctant Livi to her feet. "There are plenty of other cool guys around."

Livi shook her head disconsolately. "There

will never, ever be anyone else like Ben," she insisted, pulling a damp tissue into shreds.

Poppy recalled that she had said precisely the same thing about every boy she had ever fancied, but felt that this was possibly not the best moment to mention the fact.

"Of course there will," she said briskly. "You just need a different approach."

Livi stared at her.

"Like what?"

"Boys like an air of mystery," pronounced Poppy, who frankly didn't really know what boys liked and cared even less, but was astute enough to realise that what Livi needed right now was a plan. "You are going to have to be more remote, less available. I mean, admit it, you do sort of drool around after your boyfriends, don't you?"

Livi pouted. "I don't know what you mean," she muttered.

"Oh come off it," said Poppy. "You're always in when they phone, you never say no if they ask you out, you sit on the sidelines in freezing weather while they trundle around after some stupid ball . . ."

Livi twiddled the corner of her tissue.

"You don't understand," she protested. "You have to let boys know you care, you have to be there for them. If you don't they just up and go."

Ah, thought Poppy. So that's it. I suppose in her circumstances that attitude is understandable. I shall have to do something about that.

"Well, it's time *we* got up and went," she said firmly. "You know what a tizz old Peewit gets into if we're late for her beloved geography."

"But what am I going to do?" persisted Livi.

"For now, you are going to leave everything to me," declared Poppy, giving her a hug.

And Livi, who was used to letting Poppy lead her through life, wiped her nose on her sleeve, sniffed, nodded, and tried a watery smile. Poppy would come up with something. Poppy always did.

poppy
ponders the
problem

While Miss Plover held forth at great length about the mysteries of the glacial valley, Poppy pondered on what she could do to divert Livi's attention from unrequited love. It wasn't altogether surprising that she had a somewhat distorted view of the management of relationships. Her dad had left home three months before to live in Runcorn with an accounts clerk called Rosalie. (Poppy's mother said that any man who left his wife and child deserved Runcorn, and Poppy's father said that maybe Rosalie had charms that detracted from Runcorn's distinct lack of them.)

Livi's mum, Judy, who was very arty and a little temperamental, worked three afternoons a week for Poppy's father, keeping his paperwork up to date and remembering to water the parlour palms that adorned Reception. The rest of the time she made pottery pixies and fat little fairies and sold them at craft fairs. She had spent the weeks following her spouse's departure alternating between the depths of depression (during which she made witches and hobgoblins instead), and moments of madly demonstrative joy, when she dyed her hair bizarre colours, burnt incense cones in every corner of the house, and told anyone who would listen that she felt liberated from the constraints of marital bondage and was going to find herself at a weekend retreat in Milton Keynes.

Livi favoured the joyous moments, because whenever Poppy's mother heard that her friend Judy was going off to sit cross-legged and murmur mantras, she would insist that Livi come to stay with them at The Hollies. There she would spend the whole time being fed Spanish Chicken and Death by Chocolate, and Poppy's father would get out his camera and tell her what fine cheekbones she had. Livi, whose own father frequently failed to notice her existence, never mind her cheekbones, and whose mother's expertise in the kitchen amounted to piercing the plastic on a microwavable lasagne, considered the Fields to be the perfect family. Poppy, not for the first time, thought how unfortunate it was that not everyone was blessed with parents who were well-balanced, responsible human beings with a grasp on the important things in life.

"Poppy Field, are you listening?" Peewit fixed her with a steely stare. "I hardly think you are going to absorb the effects of glaciation on the landscapes of Europe by staring out of the window like an adolescent zombie."

"Sorry, Miss Plover." Silly old bat, thought Poppy, who considered that if a valley was already there, it was pretty pointless to spend forty-five minutes working out why. She was perfectly sure that she could stagger through life without a detailed knowledge of U-shaped valleys, pingos, or bedrock, whereas a quick glance at Livi's still-forlorn face and silently shaking shoulders suggested that someone had to do something about her self-image and fast.

And of course, since no one else seemed the slightest bit aware of the urgency of the situation, that someone would have to be Poppy.

Poppy had been sorting Livi out ever since the days when they went to Abingvale play group together. Her roller coaster ride of romance had started at the age of three and three quarters, when Darren Smythe had let her ride his red plastic fire engine and given her all the orange Smarties from his lunch box. The following day, he had transferred his allegiance to Katy Wentworth, and Poppy had found Livi hiding behind the coat pegs, crying her eyes out. She had given her a squashed custard cream from her pocket and her Paddington Bear handkerchief and told her not to cry and that Darren was stupid anyway, because he couldn't hop, couldn't wink one eye, and didn't even know his left hand from his right.

"You can be my friend instead," Poppy had said with the assertiveness for which she was to become famous. And Livi had grinned happily, slipped her hand into Poppy's, and leaned on her ever since. It suited Poppy very well. She liked to be needed.

And needed she had been. While Poppy had sailed through childhood with little more than an attack of mumps, two broken front teeth (the direct result of attempting to jump the rabbit hutch on her tricycle) and the sad death of the unwatered goldfish to disturb her, Livi had not fared quite so well. Her father, whose dedication to hard work was not quite as concentrated as his attraction to members of the opposite sex, had been fired from a variety of jobs. As a result, the Hunters, who used to live round the corner from Poppy's family in a Victorian rectory, were eventually forced to move in order to pacify the building society, who took exception to not receiving any money for months on end.

When this happened, Livi's mum, who had become very accustomed to her pine kitchen, studio at the bottom of the garden, and weekly meals at The Famished Friar, had spent several days sitting in the Fields' kitchen, weeping copiously into the potpourri, eating vast quantities of almond flapjack, and contemplating divorce. Then, just as suddenly, she had rallied, taken to playing "Stand by Your Man" on the stereo, and booked herself stalls at every craft fair within a fifty-mile radius. Sadly, the profit on pottery pixies, exquisitely crafted as they were, was not enough to save the situation, and within weeks, the Hunters had moved to a red brick Edwardian terrace near the canal. There Judy continued to churn out wizards and witches from the back bedroom, and smile through gritted teeth and tell everyone that everything would be fine, and that the crisis had brought them closer together as a couple, all the time unaware that her husband's frequent trips to Runcorn were not to search for new employment but to woo the radiant Rosalie.

Poppy had pacified Livi over the frequent absences of her father and the attendant bad moods of her mother, had lavished her with gifts when Mrs. Hunter abruptly cut her allowance by two thirds, had invited her home to tea on the days when Livi's mum was too distraught to cook and had constantly reassured her that most men (Poppy's own father excepted, of course) had mid-life crises and that Mr. Hunter would undoubtedly return home, full of remorse, very shortly; but in Poppy's opinion, the area that needed real attention was the chaos of Livi's own love life.

The trouble with Livi, thought Poppy as Peewit droned on about bedrock, was that she was so desperate to be loved that she took the simplest of gestures, such as a boy sharing his packet of beef and onion crisps with her, as an indication of undying devotion. There was no question of her playing hard to get—once she had decided that this time it was the Real Thing, and started calling herself Olivia again, because it sounded more sophisticated, she would become the devoted slave of the current object of her adoration. The summer before, when she had fallen for Paul Roberts, who was the shining light of the tennis team, she had borrowed Poppy's racquet and began standing by the tennis courts, swinging it hopefully. Todd Chambers, who Poppy thought was the best of the lot, had signed up for the school Adventure weekend, so Livi, who hated mud and until then had considered that the great outdoors was for looking at through double glazing, had gone along too in high hopes of two days of romance on a rock face. She had come home on the school minibus with a sprained ankle, a streaming cold, and three pairs of torn leggings. Todd, meanwhile, had gone home with Charlotte Gilbey in her dad's silver BMW.

What Livi needed, Poppy decided, was either a project so absorbing as to divert Livi's attention right away from the opposite sex (and even Poppy had to admit that this would be hard to achieve) or else someone whose devotion to Livi would be unstinting, who would be there for her through thick and thin until the time came when Livi was the one to grow weary.

Poppy would have liked to have given the matter her undivided attention there and then, but Miss Plover was bringing the geography lesson to a close, and Poppy had another pressing matter to attend to in her free period.

She had to see the headmaster and give him the news of her latest plan for transforming the life of the school.

poppy puts forward a plan

Mr. Graham Golding had been head-master of Bellborough Court School for a very long time and was somewhat set in his ways, a characteristic that Poppy was determined to change. Admittedly, up to now she had had only very modest success. Her suggestion that the school's annual Three Arts Festival should be replaced by a Eurovision-style song contest had been turned down out of hand; her request for a complaints box outside the staff room had been referred to the board of governors who had sighed and smiled in amusement and filed it under Pending; and her design for a new school uniform, while receiving a great deal of approval for its artistic merit from Mrs. Willis, the head of art, had got no further than page three of her project file. But, she reflected as she made her way across the hall to the headmaster's study, this latest idea of hers was so brilliant, she knew that even old Gee-Gee would not be able to resist it. After all, he was always telling his students about the importance of compassion and caring in our modern world, and how they must pull together for the good of everyone at Bellborough Court. Poppy was certain that her scheme would enhance school life enormously.

Bellborough Court was not a major public school; it was not even a minor public school. It was, in fact, simply an ex-grammar school which, when faced with the choice of going independent or being sucked into the comprehensive system had opted for the former, given itself the motto *"Absque Labore Nihil,"* which meant "Without Labour Nothing"—and which several mothers were heard to say would have been more appropriate over the doorway of a maternity hospital than a provincial seat of learning—and started charging parents exorbitant fees for the privilege of having their offspring educated there. Poppy's father, who had to pay the fees, couldn't really see what was wrong with Lee Hill, their local comprehensive, but Poppy's mother had insisted that only the best was good enough for her daughters, and if Mr. Field occasionally questioned her interpretation of the word best, he was far too accustomed to deferring to his adored wife to actually say anything.

Poppy knocked on Mr. Golding's door and waited.

"Come in!"

Gee-Gee, a tall, slender man with greying hair and a nose that appeared to have been attached to his face as an afterthought, looked up questioningly from his paperwork as Poppy entered, wearing what she hoped was a pleasant but not too forward smile.

"Good afternoon, sir," she said.

"Good afternoon, Poppy. Have a seat," said Mr. Golding, replacing the top on his fountain pen with meticulous care. "Now what can I do for you?"

"Well, actually sir, it is more what I can do for you," said Poppy eagerly.

"Really?" said Mr. Golding, the faintest shadow of a smile twitching at the corners of his mouth.

Poppy nodded. "I've had this mega brilliant idea for the school magazine," she said. "You see, sir, what we have to do is bring it up to date, make it more reader-friendly, attack the real issues of the day." She had gleaned this last phrase from the *Guardian* and was rather pleased with it. She took her job as magazine coordinator for Year Nine very seriously.

"Well, Poppy, I think you have made a good contribution already—your piece on the need for more ramps in public places was most edifying—if a little ungrammatical," he added wryly.

"Oh that," said Poppy dismissively. "This is far more important. I want to run an agony column."

Had Poppy announced that she would be including nude portraits of every member of staff, Gee-Gee could not have looked more horrified.

"Oh no, Poppy, that is simply not a possibility," said Mr. Golding emphatically. "The *Bellborough Bulletin* is not the vehicle for downmarket trivia. It is there to convey to parents, ex-pupils, and other interested parties, news of the achievements of the past year, sporting successes, dramatic productions . . ."

"But don't you see, sir, all *that* is trivia, compared with people's personal anxieties? The way I see it is that people could write in with their problems, and I could give advice on the best way of . . ."

Mr. Golding appeared to be stricken with a sudden fit of coughing.

"Poppy, we have PSE classes in which pupils can talk about their worries and . . ."

"Oh, come off it, sir!" expostulated Poppy. "Would you start chatting about your parents' divorce or your dad's redundancy and stuff like that in class? But you see, people could write in under made-up names to my column . . ."

"There isn't going to be any column, Poppy," said Mr. Golding. "I'm sorry. I am sure your motives are most altruistic, but it just is not on. And besides, I hardly think that you have sufficient experience of life to begin counselling others."

Poppy looked a little hurt at this reflection on her expertise. "I am very good at sorting things out," she said. "Most problems have very simple solutions, if only people will keep calm and think it all through." She paused. "You could look on it as work experience, sir," she added brightly. "I'm going to be an agony aunt when I leave school."

"Indeed?" commented Gee-Gee. "Well, Poppy, I am sorry, but my answer is still no. No column."

Poppy sighed and turned for the door.

"Oh, before you go, Poppy . . ." Mr. Golding waved a hand towards the chair. Poppy sat down again.

"Everything all right at home?"

Why, Poppy wondered, when you come up with any idea that goes even slightly against the grain, do adults immediately assume it springs from some disaster on the domestic front?

"Fine, thank you," said Poppy.

"Mother well?" Poppy nodded. Her mother was never ill because she took multivitamins, ginseng, and cod liver oil and only used organic vegetables.

"And your father—away on business a lot, is he?"

Poppy looked puzzled and shook her head.

"No, sir—why?"

Mr. Golding looked a little flustered.

"Oh nothing, no, nothing of consequence." He fiddled with his pen. "I dropped him a line a few weeks ago and when I didn't hear back I assumed he must be out of town."

Poppy shrugged.

"Maybe the letter went astray," she offered.

"Indeed so," said Mr. Golding. "Indeed so. I will write again."

"Was it important, sir? Shall I take a letter home?"

Mr. Golding looked at her eager face, opened his mouth, and shut it again.

"Sir?"

"No, Poppy, it wasn't important," he assured her. "I'll write again. You may go now."

Poppy stood up.

"Yes, Poppy?"

"You wouldn't like to reconsider about the column?"

"No, Poppy, I would not."

"I think, sir," said Poppy gravely, "that you are making a big mistake."

"That," said Mr. Golding, "is something I am simply going to have to live with."

poppy lays
a plot

Poppy was very wounded that Mr. Golding had not viewed her suggestion in a more favourable light, but she was not one to dwell on negatives, and as she stuffed her books into her kitbag, she reflected that she would simply have to think of another way of ensuring that as many people as possible could benefit from her counselling skills.

She might well approach the *Leehampton Echo* and offer to write a teenage agony page. Or two. But first, she had to get Livi back on an even keel.

Her friend was nowhere to be seen in the locker room, and Poppy assumed she had already gone to the bus stop. But as she ran over to the school gates, she saw Livi leaning against the wall outside the music block, deep in conversation with Luke Cunningham. Livi's expertise on the piano and oboe had won her the Leehampton music scholarship to Bellborough, and Luke was the school's best flautist, so Poppy guessed they were talking music. Livi was listening intently to whatever Luke was saying, and he was, as usual, looking worried.

Poppy had always felt rather sorry for Luke Cunningham. He wore a permanently anxious expression on his pale face, even when he was playing in the school orchestra or collecting yet another cup for winning the inter-school chess competition. Not that you could expect him to be particularly cheerful. On a frosty morning about a year before, Luke's mother had left home early to fetch his dad from Heathrow airport, and somewhere on the M25 her car had hit a patch of black ice and skidded across the central reservation into the path of an oncoming lorry. Luke had told Poppy that the police said his mum would have been killed instantly.

"I think that's meant to help," he had said with tears in his eyes. "But it doesn't."

Poppy, who was never usually at a loss for words, had found for the first time in her life that she simply didn't know what to say. So she had put her hand on Luke's arm and when he had sniffed and said he was sorry, she had told him not to be silly and that if ever he wanted to talk, he could. From time to time since then, he would start to say something to her, and then stop and Poppy would begin to say, "I do understand," and then she would stop too, because she was at heart honest and knew that she couldn't possibly begin to understand what Luke must be going through. She wished there was something she could do to make him smile more.

He could be quite good-looking if he tried harder, thought Poppy. If he got a decent haircut, instead of letting his sandy-coloured hair flop around his eyes, and if he got a more trendy pair of specs, it would make a big difference. And he should be putting propolis cream on his acne too, she thought. Or tea tree oil. Poppy was very up on alternative therapies because she reckoned that when she became an agony aunt that would be just the sort of thing people would want to know about and it was never too early to start researching.

She supposed that not having a mum meant you had no one to give you advice. Luke had that lost look about him that suggested he needed someone to make a real fuss of him. She sighed. He was even worse off than Livi; Livi might miss her dad like crazy, but at least he was alive and would turn up again sometime, while Luke's mum was gone for good.

Livi and Luke. Luke and Livi! It was brilliant. Their names even sounded good together. It was the perfect solution. Livi could pour all her affection on someone who really needed it, and Luke would be so thrilled to have a regular girlfriend that he would never dump her. It was obvious he liked her because he had been talking to her for at least three minutes and lengthy conversations were not something Luke Cunningham was usually into.

Luke and Livi. She repeated their names like a mantra in her head. She couldn't imagine why she hadn't thought of it before. It was the ideal relationship, just waiting to happen. Now all Poppy had to do was make absolutely sure that it did.

livi comes
clean

"**W**hat were you talking to Luke about?" asked Poppy casually, grabbing the handrail of the school bus as it lurched onto the bypass.

"Oh, nothing," said Livi, blushing slightly and turning to look out of the window.

I see, thought Poppy. This is promising.

"He's a really nice guy, isn't he?" said Poppy encouragingly. "I really like him," she added, knowing that her good opinion would carry a lot of weight with the impressionable Livi.

"You do?" said Livi in surprise, turning to face her.

"Oh yes," enthused Poppy. "He's a really good sort."

"That's great," said Livi thoughtfully. "I'm pleased."

"Why?" said Poppy slyly.

CHAPTER SIX

"Oh, no reason," said Livi. Poppy felt very satisfied. She knew full well that with her approval, Livi would feel free to fall for Luke.

Poppy's unspoken hope that talk of Luke had driven all thoughts of the obnoxious Ben from Livi's mind was dashed as the bus turned off the bypass into Ecton Lane.

"I've had this great idea," she said confidingly. "I'm going to write Ben a letter, and take it round to his house and then . . ."

"And give him the satisfaction of seeing you grovel? No way!" protested Poppy emphatically. "Listen, Livi, from now on you have to take a different approach. You have to be elusive and mysterious. Melissa says boys thrive on suspense," she added, to give credence to her theory.

Livi pulled a face. "Well, your sister should know, the number of boyfriends she's had! Is she still going out with Nathan?"

Poppy nodded. "Sort of—it won't last, though—their star signs are incompatible," she remarked. "But there's Jake as well now and he's really keen on her. I like him because he does my French homework for me."

Livi looked forlorn. "French is Ben's best subject," she moaned. "He says—used to say—my lack of linguistic skills was endearing."

"Patronising git!" said Poppy, who found it pretty rich that Ben, who only spoke French well because his mother came from Lyon, should sneer at someone who got straight As in all the sciences and regarded a B grade in English as a cause of deep shame. "You know your problem, don't you?" she added.

"Fat thighs and freckles," sighed Livi, tugging ineffectually at the hemline of her skirt.

"Low self-esteem," corrected Poppy, recalling the phrase from a radio phone-in her mother had been listening to and thinking it had a meaningful ring to it. "You have to believe in yourself." And I know the very guy to make you, she thought.

"What's there to believe in?" moaned Livi, tugging miserably at a strand of blond hair and glowering at her reflection in the bus window. "It's all right for you—you've got it all. Perfect skin, great hair, a body that goes in and out in all the right places and parents who adore you. How could you possibly know what it's like to be fat and ugly and unlovable?"

"Oh, Livi," exclaimed Poppy, "now you are being just plain stupid. You are not fat, you are really pretty, and just because Ben 'oh how I fancy myself' Bryant has found some other sucker to tell him he's wonderful . . ."

"It's not just Ben," admitted Livi, chewing her bottom lip. "I haven't seen Dad in ages; every time I phone he says he's really busy and he'll come down soon, but he never does. I reckon now he's got this Rosalie woman he doesn't care about me."

"Of course he does!" said Poppy briskly. "I told you—men have these mid-life crises—I'm sure your mum will entice him home."

"I don't even know that she wants him," confessed Livi miserably. "Whenever I try to talk about Dad, she either snaps at me and says, "Do you have to keep mentioning that man's name?" or else looks all wounded and asks why I am thinking about him when I've got her. Either way, I end up feeling guilty for saying anything in the first place."

Poppy sighed. Surely Mrs. Hunter knew the importance of interpersonal communication—they had done that in PSE, and Poppy had told Mrs. Joll that their family discussed everything over the supper table, a policy that never failed to bring about results. Mrs. Joll had muttered, "Well, lucky you," in what seemed to Poppy to be a somewhat unnecessary tone of voice.

"Look, Livi," she said, gathering up her bag, as the bus pulled up at the end of her road. "You want to see your dad, right?"

"I've just said so, haven't I?" said Livi.

"So—if your mum won't do anything about it, you organise it!" ordered Poppy.

"How?" said Livi.

"Simple," declared Poppy. "Make it so he has no choice but to come and see you."

"How?" repeated Livi, who was brilliant at working out Pythagoras but not so hot on innovative ideas.

Poppy sighed. "I'll think of something," she said.

poppy
makes a new
acquaintance

The neighbourhood of Great Ecton, where the Fields lived, had once been a pretty village on the Bellborough to Leehampton road. But as Leehampton expanded it had become sucked into the borough that was now what the local estate agents called "one of the more desirable areas of town" and what Poppy's grandmother called "ruined." The owners of the older stone houses had sold off large portions of their gardens, into which ambitious builders had squeezed as many modern houses as they could get away with, creating little closes with names like Manor House Court and Old Bakery Way. The fields of the old farm were now a housing estate, and down by the canal old boat sheds were being converted into overpriced restaurants with names like "The Butty" and "Barge Inn." But everyone who lived in Great Ecton still determinedly referred to "the village" in an attempt to attach some sort of superiority over the adjacent neighbourhood of Billington.

Poppy ambled down Ecton Lane, pondering on just how she could get Luke and Livi together and what method she should employ to convince Livi's father of the necessity for him to abandon the wretched Rosalie and return to the bosom of his pining family. She was mulling over the possibility of writing to Mr. Hunter and telling him that Livi was refusing all food and wasting away, when a somewhat quavery voice interrupted her musings.

"Might I trouble you for an elastic band?"

Poppy turned. Sitting on a wooden bench outside the primary school was an exceedingly thin old woman with a weather-beaten face as wrinkled as overused wrapping paper. At her feet was a rather battered holdall and two carrier bags. She wore a pair of bright red cord trousers, a shocking-pink anorak, and a green felt hat adorned with a rather weary-looking feather. She looked like a very crinkled radish.

"Pardon?" said Poppy politely.

"An elastic band, dear—I just wondered if you had one—or even two." The voice was surprisingly gentle and well-modulated. "It's just that this anorak—only 50p dear, from the Oxfam, rather fetching I thought—well, anyway the sleeves, you see . . ." She waggled stick-thin arms in Poppy's direction. "They are a little on the overlong side, if you take my meaning."

Poppy scrabbled in her school bag and pulled an elastic band off her biology folder and another from her pencil case.

"Will these do?" she enquired.

"Capital," cried the old lady, clapping her hands in delight. "Many thanks."

She slipped the elastic bands over her wrists, hitched up the sleeves, and admired the effect.

"Oh, I'm Ada, by the way," she said. "And you are?"

"Poppy Field," said Poppy, shaking the proffered weather-beaten hand. "I haven't seen you before. Where do you live?"

The old lady chuckled. "Here, there, and

pretty much everywhere," she said. "I travel," she added, with the dignity of one who cruises the Caribbean twice yearly.

"What, you mean, you're a tramp?" enquired Poppy disbelievingly.

"No, I most certainly do not mean that I am a tramp," snorted the old woman. "Do I look like a tramp?" Poppy refrained from replying. "I merely choose to move around. And now, if you will excuse me, it is time for tea." And so saying, she removed an overripe banana from her jacket pocket.

"But where do you sleep?" persisted Poppy.

The old woman paused in mid-nibble. "Last night, in a bus shelter. The night before in a rather convenient barn. Sometimes"—she hugged herself with glee—"in a hostel—hot shower, soup and rolls, and, best of all, newspapers to read. I do enjoy the *Guardian*, you know. One must keep abreast."

"But that's terrible!" cried Poppy. "What about tonight?"

The old lady shrugged. "Wherever," she said. "I am considering the possibilities."

Poppy took a decision.

"You must come home with me," she said. "It'll be dark soon and it's getting cold. We've oodles of space—you can have a bath, and my mum is a brill cook, and . . ."

The old lady shook her head adamantly.

"Very kind, dear, but not on," she said. "Wouldn't be right."

"Of course it would," declared Poppy. "Come on, it's only round the corner."

The old lady shook her head.

"Best not," she said. Then her face softened. "But thanks anyway."

"Just stay there," ordered Poppy. "I'll be right back." Poppy had already decided that Ada was not going to sleep one more night on the streets. Not if she had anything to do with it.

"Mum, listen—there's this old woman and she hasn't got anywhere to sleep and I thought she could come here and have a bath and . . ."

Mrs. Field turned from the table, where she was doing something enormously artistic with two bent twigs, a candle, and a peace lily, and said, "Steady on—what old woman?"

"She's a tramp—well, not a tramp, a traveller, and I thought she could . . ."

Poppy's mother held up an immaculately manicured hand and two sizeable diamonds twinkled in the light.

"Stop right there, sweetheart," she ordered. "We are not getting involved with those sort of people and that's final." She took a step back and surveyed her table decoration critically.

"But Mum, she sleeps rough and I'm sure she doesn't eat enough. She's ever so thin."

Her mother shrugged. "People like that bring it on themselves," she declared. "Just don't get involved, Poppy."

Poppy glared at her mother.

"That is so uncharitable," she shouted. "Don't you care about the underprivileged?"

"Of course I do," protested Mrs. Field, tweaking a lily leaf. "I do my bit you know—I do the door-to-door collections for Shelter and Oxfam and then there's my charity tea for the church— but it's quite another thing dragging smelly old women in off the street."

"She's not smelly," said Poppy. "And how would you like it if you were homeless?"

Poppy's mother smiled and patted her freshly coiffeured hair which managed to retain its shiny blackness with considerable help from one of Fringe Affairs' more expensive colour treatments.

"Well, I wouldn't be, would I, because our sort of people see to it that we are not. Now, should I put this on the hall table or in the sitting room?"

And carefully balancing her floral masterpiece in one hand, she went through to the hall.

Poppy watched her, a puzzled frown on her face. Then she opened the fridge, took out two yoghurts, a packet of cheese and several slices of hickory-roast ham. She cut a wedge of her mother's famous coffee and walnut sponge cake, and, grabbing two apples from the fruit bowl, slipped out of the back door.

The bench was empty. The only sign that Ada had ever been there was a banana skin lying amid the nettles and dandelions that grew by the school fence. Poppy ran to the corner of the road and peered up and down the hill. Nothing.

Poppy felt cheated. She was all in favour of championing good causes, but it was very disappointing when your good cause disappeared before you could bestow your generosity on it.

Biting into the cake which she had intended to form part of Ada's supper, she ambled back up the road. She did hope Ada would be all right. She seemed very old to be wandering around on her own. Perhaps she should phone the police and they could give her a warm room for the night. That would be a good idea. If Poppy couldn't play the part of the ministering angel herself she could at least make sure that someone else did.

Pleased with her solution, Poppy quickened her pace and as she rounded the corner, she saw her father standing on the driveway of their house, his expensive cashmere coat slung casually over his shoulders, fondly stroking the bonnet of his racing green Jaguar.

"Hi, Dad!" called Poppy. "You're home early."

Leo Field started as if out of a dream and looked at his daughter.

"What? Oh, hello, sweetheart," he said, his

dark brown eyes lighting up with pleasure at the sight of his daughter.

"Making love to your car again?" teased Poppy. It was a family joke that if the Field family were threatened by flood, fire, or famine, Mr. Field would be hard pressed to decide whether to save them or his beloved Jag.

Her father smiled a weary smile, bestowed another affectionate gaze on his car and turned towards the house. Poppy thought he looked rather grey. His shoulders were drooping and his jacket, normally pressed with immaculate precision, was crumpled and creased. He took a tube of extra-strong mints from his trouser pocket and offered her one.

"You OK, Dad?" she asked, slipping a Minty-Oh into her mouth.

He looked at her for a long time, sucking on his sweet. Then he took a deep breath and smiled.

"Yes, Poppy, love, I'm fine."

"Good. Oh, by the way, I saw old Gee-Gee— Mr. Golding—today," she added. Mr. Field looked at her sharply.

"It's OK," she said reassuringly, "I wasn't in trouble. Only he said he had written to you and it must have gone astray."

Mr. Field's shoulders appeared to droop even more and he closed his eyes briefly.

"Oh," he said. "Fine."

"Dad—are you sure you're OK?" said Poppy anxiously.

Mr. Field smiled broadly and put an arm around her shoulders.

"Of course," he said cheerfully. "Never better."

Poppy was satisfied.

"That's good," she said. "Because tonight we're sorting the holiday and Melly's party."

Her father stopped in his tracks, closed his eyes, looked heavenward and took another deep breath.

"Not another one of your mother's organisational evenings?" he said pleadingly.

Poppy giggled.

"That's right," she said.

Usually her dad would have pulled a funny face, said something about going to ground in his darkroom to print negatives until hostilities were over and laughed it off. Instead, he ran his fingers through his greying hair, rubbed his hand across the back of his neck, and said in a dull sort of voice, "That's all I need right now."

And for some reason that left Poppy with a very uncomfortable feeling in her stomach.

boy talk

Poppy marched into the hall, intending to phone the police and instigate a full-scale search for Ada. She was prevented from putting this plan into action by her sister, who was sitting on the bottom stair gripping the receiver with white knuckles and looking far from happy.

"That is the most stupid thing I have ever heard in my entire life!" she stormed. There was a pause. "I am not your personal property. Well, if that's the way you feel, you can take a running jump! Good-bye!" Melly slammed the receiver back on the slimline phone, which jumped halfway across the hall table.

"That told them," commented Poppy wryly as her sister flounced up the stairs two at a time.

"Oh, it's you," said Melly, looking over her shoulder. "Honestly, I have had it with boys, I truly have!"

Poppy felt that the day that her sister

disassociated herself from the opposite sex would be the day hell froze over, but she refrained from commenting.

"Who is it this time? Nathan? Jake?" queried Poppy, following her on to the landing.

Poppy's mother emerged from the bedroom carrying a pile of magazines.

"You haven't fallen out with Jake, have you, darling?" she asked her elder daughter, and Poppy could not help but notice the slightly hopeful tone in her voice. She knew her mother favoured Nathan Meade, who wore Armani shirts and Ralph Lauren polos and whose father was MP for Leehampton and Kettleborough and let the East Midlands Opera perform in a marquee on his vast lawn. Nathan was at the local agricultural college, preparing to follow in his father's footsteps. Mrs. Field, who had been invited to one of the Meades' famous musical soirées the previous summer took great delight in ensuring that all her friends knew that Melissa was going out with the heir to Meade Hall Farm. The fact that she was also going out with Jake Winters, whose father was a plumber and whose mother worked on the checkout in the local Spar shop, she failed to mention to anyone. Jake was at art college and frequently made pin money by chalking brilliant pictures onto the paving stones in the Market Square, an activity that Poppy's mother thought too downmarket for words. There were the odd occasions when Poppy wondered whether her mother was just the tiniest little bit snobbish.

"Fallen out with Jake? No, of course I haven't," declared Melly, and her mother's face fell. "He's a perfect angel."

"I don't think," said Poppy as they went into Melly's bedroom and shut the door, "that Mum is madly enthusiastic about Jake."

Poppy had on several occasions listened to her mother's reservations about what she called, "a six-foot happening with a stud in his left nostril and unruly hair that could do with some immediate attention from Candice at Fringe Affairs." She remembered the evening when Melly had come home from the jazz club and burst into the sitting room, dragging her new-found love behind her.

"This is Jake and it is OK for him to crash here tonight, isn't it?" she had asked.

Poppy, who had been listening to Blur on her headphones at the time, saw her mother's face adopt its "How awfully nice to meet you" expression while her mouth opened and closed like a goldfish. She had wrenched her earphones off in time to catch "Make yourself at home" and hear Jake say "Nice one" and drift off to the spare bedroom. Poppy had since noticed that a well-thumbed copy of *Teenage Years Without Trauma* had reappeared on her mother's bedside table.

"Mum likes Nathan best because he speaks nicely and tells her how young she looks," observed Melly. "But now he's saying that if Jake comes to my eighteenth, he won't, which is so pathetic it's unreal. He thinks just because he sent me two dozen red roses for Valentine's Day, he owns me."

Poppy pondered the two huge vases of blooms on Melly's windowsill.

"Maybe he is so desperately in love with you that he can't stand the competition," she offered. "Perhaps he is consumed with jealousy."

"Tough," said Melissa. "I am no one's possession; I belong only to me."

Poppy made a mental note of that comment, which she thought sounded particularly pertinent. Melissa had a very acute turn of phrase at times.

"Besides," added Melissa, pouting her lips and applying two liberal coats of amber lipstick, "he'll come round—I know how to handle him."

She picked up a hairbrush and began rhythmically brushing her immaculately bobbed hair.

"And who do you like best—really?" asked Poppy, idly trying on a pair of Melissa's earrings.

Melly shrugged. "Depends what I want them for really," she said. "I mean, Nathan is great socially—for parties and balls and stuff. He's invited me to the Spring Ball next month," she added.

"Wow!" Poppy was impressed. "You'll be in *Harpers* and *Tatler*," she said enviously.

"The Meades know heaps of important people, and Nathan thinks I'm wonderful, which helps," added Melly.

"So you like him better than Jake?" questioned Poppy, viewing her earlobes with some satisfaction.

Melissa sighed.

"I don't know—Jake's pretty much a dead loss on the party scene, and he's always broke and has positively no dress sense. But then again, he's really sweet and I can talk for hours and hours about absolutely everything—he's got this incredible mind," she said.

"His body isn't bad either," said Poppy.

"Poppy!" giggled Melissa "I thought you didn't concern yourself with such things—my little sister must be growing up."

Poppy laughed good-naturedly and stuck her tongue out at her sister.

"But you are going to have to choose sometime, aren't you?" reasoned Poppy. "I mean, you can't keep them both on a string forever."

"Why not?" asked Melly. "Treat them mean and keep them keen—that's the rule with boys. You can have those earrings if you want them," she added.

"Really?" said Poppy.

"They're only imitation junk, not real silver," said Melissa. "Take them."

Poppy pocketed them with glee.

"So are they really jealous of each other—Nathan and Jake, I mean?" queried Poppy.

Melissa shrugged. "Nathan reckons Jake doesn't deserve me," she said with a glimmer of self-satisfaction, "and Jake says Nathan is a shallow-minded bigot." She plucked a stray hair from her left eyebrow. "Not that it matters much, because Vicki and I are off to Oz soon and they'll both have to manage without me, won't they?"

"I suppose," said Poppy doubtfully. Perhaps, she thought, Jake would pine a lot and Poppy could comfort him. The thought of offering Jake Winters a shoulder to cry on suddenly held a great deal of appeal for Poppy.

granny jay has some news

Poppy was not pleased with her phone call to Leehampton Police. She had reported that Ada had gone missing from the bench where Poppy had left her and had explained that in her opinion she was in need of a hot bath and some substantial food, and the officer at the other end had spluttered and asked what relation Poppy was to the missing person. When Poppy explained that they had only just met but that Ada needed accommodation and she thought the police should send a patrol car and take her somewhere warm, the officer appeared to be stricken with a fit of choking. He then spouted a lot about not being able to care for every vagrant in the district, and if Ada was doing no one any harm and had departed from the bench of her own free will, there was nothing they could do. Poppy told him quite firmly that she would be writing to her MP, the Prime Minister, and, quite possibly, the Queen, and rang off.

There was no doubt about it, she told herself, people simply didn't care enough for one another. Perhaps when she had made a lot of money from being an agony aunt, she would open a hostel for the down and out. She could be a sort of Mother Theresa of Leehampton. The idea held a certain charm.

Granny Jay often came for supper on Friday evenings, and when Poppy clattered downstairs, the sight of a knitted hat in varying shades of purple and a blue plastic mac of uncertain age draped haphazardly over the banister suggested she had arrived.

Sure enough, she was sitting at the scrubbed pine kitchen table, enveloped in a floral apron and chopping a pile of vegetables with a fury that suggested she bore a personal grudge against each individual carrot.

"I've never heard anything like it in all my born days," Poppy heard her say as she pushed open the kitchen door.

"Hi Gran!" said Poppy. "Never heard anything like what?"

Poppy's mother turned from the table where she was peeling pears.

"Granny Jay is in one of her frames of mind," she said, winking at Poppy.

Granny Jay's frames of mind were well known, not only to her immediate family but to her neighbours, the congregation and clergy of St. Nicholas Church (where she was prone to kick up a fuss if they sang hymns to the wrong tune or failed to keep the brasses polished to her exacting standards), and, most of all, to anyone unwise enough to suggest that perhaps, since she had just had her seventy-seventh birthday, she might like to take things a little easier.

"The devil makes work for idle hands," she would declare and continued delivering church magazines and organising the Over Sixties and going to her oil painting class and telling anyone who would pay attention that politicians had got it all wrong and it was never like this in her day.

Once Granny Jay got an idea in her head, she would hold forth on the subject at considerable length, accompanied by a great deal of pursing of the lips and loud sniffing, until suddenly, having got the matter off her chest, she would sit back, say, "What can't be cured must be endured," and carry on as if nothing had happened. Those around her took hours to recover from the experience.

"There you are then, Poppy my love," she said, standing up and planting a damp kiss on Poppy's forehead. In addition to speaking in proverbs and doing her own thing, Granny Jay was also inclined to state the obvious. "Are you warm enough in that hairband of a skirt?"

She crossed to the cooker and dumped the massacred vegetables into a pan.

"I'm fine, Gran," laughed Poppy. "What are you on about now?"

Granny Jay pulled herself up to her full four feet eleven inches. "I am not *on* about anything," she said. "I was just saying that if there is one sort of person I have no time for, it's do-gooders."

Poppy and her mother exchanged amused glances. In fact, there were several types of people for whom Granny Jay declared she had no time, including nearly everyone who wrote for the national newspapers, women who didn't keep their net curtains washed, and anyone who dared to call her "my duck," which tended to include every shopkeeper in Leehampton.

Since it seemed unlikely that Granny Jay was ever going to get to the point, Mrs. Field decided to elaborate.

"Granny is upset because Charley Rust is moving from Canal End."

Poppy looked aghast.

"Charley? Moving?" she said. "He can't move, he's my social history project," she added, as if this fact alone were enough to guarantee his ongoing habitation of the cottage next door to her grandmother.

Charley Rust was eighty-six years old and had lived beside the Leehampton canal ever since the days when he was the canal's lock-keeper and Poppy was using him for her "Townspeople then and now" project. She had already spent two afternoons drinking tea and eating buttered buns and listening to Charley's reminiscences about the days of coal barges and horses on the towpath and felt that a few more sessions should ensure her of a good grade. She couldn't be doing with him moving now.

"I didn't say he *was* moving," corrected Granny Jay. "I said they wanted him to. Trouble is, he'll probably go. He hasn't got the sense he was born with, silly old fool."

Charley and Granny Jay had known each other for sixty years, most of which had been spent locked in argument on every topic from whether it would rain the following day to the best way of growing radishes in clay soil. She called him a silly old fool, and he called her a stubborn old bat, but when Charley had had bronchitis, Granny Jay was the one who appeared with onion soup, Epsom salts for his bath, and eucalyptus for his chest; and when her beloved cat, Topsy, had died, it was Charley who dug the grave in the tiny back garden and held her hand and pretended to believe her when she said that of course she wasn't crying, it was just a very chill wind. On occasions they would sit by one another's fires, and Granny Jay would talk about her George and Charley would recount tales of his Gladys and then they would say, "God rest their souls," and have a cocoa and some of Granny Jay's sticky chocolate cake.

Over all the years that Poppy's parents had been trying to persuade Granny Jay to leave the cottage and move somewhere nicer (Poppy's mother because she didn't like telling her country club friends about her humble origins and Poppy's father because he was genuinely concerned that Granny Jay needed full central heating and a burglar alarm), Poppy's grandmother had said that the cottage did her nicely, thank you very much, she'd reared two children in it, and besides she couldn't leave, because how would Charley manage without her, the silly old fool?

"Social Services think that Charley would be better moving to Victoria House," explained Poppy's mother. "And you must say, Ma, it does make sense. I mean, he's not getting any younger and he's none too steady on his feet. What if he fell into the canal?"

Granny Jay looked at her in amazement.

"Charley Rust fall into the canal? Saints preserve us, he never fell in when he worked there day and night—why would he start now?" She moved a boiling saucepan from the stove. "I'll be having words with that Mortimer woman about this."

"Who?" said Poppy, sticking her finger in the bolognese sauce and licking it appreciatively.

"Phyllis Mortimer," said Granny Jay. "If she hadn't gone running to Social Services none of this would have happened. Still, if he will have Meals on Wheels when I'd already offered my fish pie and my hotpot, what does he expect?"

It transpired that Mrs. Mortimer, who delivered a hot lunch to Charley three days a week, had been worried about the state of his cottage with its ill-fitting window frames, dangerous stairs, and fraying carpets, and had alerted Social Services, which in due course had offered him a room at Victoria House, colour television, three hot meals a day, and two outings a month.

"Sounds wonderful," said Poppy's mother. Granny Jay shot her a glance that could have stopped a guided missile in its tracks.

"Wonderful? Being shoved in an institution? Giving up your freedom? I'll have something to say to his Jennifer when I see her."

"Who's Jennifer?" asked Poppy, ushering her grandmother into the dining room.

"Charley's daughter—lives in London," hissed Granny Jay, in tones that suggested one could expect little good of anyone living in the capital. "Better she should have him with her than pack him off into some home where they'll leave him in an armchair to die." Her voice wobbled.

"You really will miss him, won't you, Gran?" said Poppy gently, taking her grandmother's hand.

Her grandmother smiled and said, "Do you know, I rather think I shall. We go back a long time, Charley and me, a very long time." She gave herself a little shake. "Silly old fool."

"It's not far," said Poppy. "We'll go and see him together."

"Sherry, Beryl?" Poppy's father poked his head round the door.

"I shouldn't," said Granny Jay.

"But you will," said Poppy with a grin.

another plan by poppy

Once everyone had been served, Poppy announced that she had something to say.

"I had this mega brilliant plan today. I know what we can do about Granny Jay."

"Excuse me," said her grandmother, who was a little flushed following the sherry. "I was not aware I needed anything doing about me."

"Look, Gran," said Poppy, "you can't stay in the cottage forever."

"And why not?" Her grandmother drew back her shoulders, prodded a wayward pea, and looked offended.

"It's just not sensible, especially if Charley's going, and I thought"—Poppy looked around to ensure that she had the full attention of her parents and sister—"we can put you in the double garage," she concluded triumphantly.

Four faces stared at Poppy.

"The garage?" stuttered Granny Jay. "The child's lost her senses. I am not a vehicle."

"Oh, we convert it first, of course," laughed Poppy. "I've seen these plans in Mum's *Home From Home*. You take off the doors, build a big bay window, put in a door, and everything. It would be so neat," she added.

Mrs. Field looked first at Poppy and then at her husband and then at Granny Jay.

"What about the cars?" queried Mr. Field.

"Simple," said Poppy. "We build a new garage the other side of the house, where the big rose bed is. You're always moaning about having to prune them."

"You know," her mother remarked thoughtfully, "that's not such a bad idea."

Mr. Field looked worried.

Poppy looked pleased.

"I don't do bad ideas," she said. "It would be lovely. And the workshop at the back could be made into a shower room. What about it, Gran?"

They all waited for Granny Jay to launch into a diatribe about how she was staying in her cottage till she came out in a box and how what was good enough for her George was good enough for her, but it didn't happen. She merely pursed her lips, dabbed her mouth delicately with her table napkin and said softly, "And what do you think of the idea, Leo?"

Mr. Field, who had been pushing spaghetti round his plate half-heartedly for some minutes, leaned back in his chair.

"Well, of course, Ma, it would be absolutely tremendous to have you up here, and I do agree that the cottage is hardly suitable, but it would be quite an expense to do all the conversion work and . . ."

"Oh, Leo, really," said his wife. "We wouldn't begrudge spending the money for Ma."

Mr. Field chewed his bottom lip.

"It's a neat idea," said Melissa. "Nathan's parents have just turned the stables into a gym and sauna."

"There you are then," asserted Poppy's mother, quite obviously delighted that they would be following in such illustrious footsteps.

"It's an expensive enterprise," began Mr. Field.

"No, it's not," said Melissa, who was going to do economics at university. "If Gran sells the cottage, the money will more than pay for the conversion."

Her father perked up. "Of course, the cottage could take months to sell," he said, "but if we are still—I mean, when it does, then that would seem a very good idea."

Mrs. Field clapped her hands in delight and Poppy and Melly grinned at one another.

"Isn't that great, Gran?" enthused Poppy.

Her grandmother smiled at her. "It's very sweet of you to bother about your old gran," she said noncommitally.

"So that's settled then," announced Poppy with satisfaction.

Granny Jay smiled again, inclined her head, but said nothing. She just watched her son-in-law's face as he began pushing the food around his plate once more.

mr. field loses his cool

"Now we can talk about holidays?" asked Poppy's mother over dessert. "We really must make the booking, Leo—have you decided? Is it to be a villa in Tuscany or that little hotel in Sorrento?"

Leo, who had given up all pretence of eating his spaghetti and was now toying with poached pears, put down his spoon.

"Do we have to decide right now?" he asked wearily. "I mean, there's no point rushing into it."

Mrs Field sighed impatiently and tapped her scarlet fingernails on the table.

"Oh, really, you've been saying that since Christmas," she said. "If we don't decide soon, the best accommodations will all be taken."

"Well then," snapped Mr. Field, "we shall just have to have second-best, won't we?"

"Leo!" protested his wife.

"Dad!" cried Poppy and Melissa in unison.

Granny Jay narrowed her eyes and looked thoughtful.

"Sorry," said Mr. Field, holding up his hand in apology. "Sorry. But we've got Melly's party to pay for and—well, things are just a bit tight at the moment."

Mrs. Field looked at him in astonishment.

"Tight?" she repeated. "How do you mean, tight?"

Mrs. Field spoke with the confusion of one who makes a weekly trip to the hole in the wall and grabs a fistful of notes without paying the slightest heed to how they got there in the first place.

"The thing is," Poppy's father began and stopped. "Look, I've got a big meeting next Friday and if that goes well, we can book the holiday then. How's that?"

"What meeting?" asked Mrs. Field.

"Oh, er—just sales stuff," said Poppy's father. "But I will know—I will know more about suitable dates after that," he said hurriedly.

Granny Jay sniffed and threw him a penetrating look. Mr. Field began paying a great deal of attention to his half-eaten pear.

"I suppose," sighed Mrs. Field somewhat sulkily, "it will have to do. I mean, I really need a holiday—I've been rushed off my feet. It's at least three months since we had a weekend away."

Poppy's father said nothing.

"Now, about my party," interrupted Melissa. "The disco is going to set up in the conservatory and the food will be in here and we'll dance in the sitting room and the hall. And we need to buy those big garden flares to put either side of the driveway and I thought we should have loads of helium balloons tied to the gate. Oh, and I booked a vocalist, too—everyone has them these days. OK?" she added, beaming at everyone.

Her father pushed back his chair and flung down his table napkin.

"Oh fine, Melly, absolutely fine!" he shouted. "While you're at it, why not go and book the band of the flaming Grenadier Guards to escort your guests up the drive? Why not have the whole house redecorated for the event? After all, it's only money isn't it? And we all know Dad will cough up, don't we?"

The outburst from the normally mild Mr. Field was so unexpected that no one moved.

"Dad?" said Poppy tentatively.

Melissa looked horror-struck and merely stared at her father.

Mrs. Field paused in mid chew.

Granny Jay was the first to recover. "I'll put the kettle on," she announced. Granny Jay was of the mind that there was nothing that couldn't be put right by a strong cup of Darjeeling.

"Dad?" Melly stood up, her blue eyes brimming with tears. "I thought you wanted me to have a nice eighteenth—before A levels start and everything. And there is only a week to go. And I will be going away for nine months," she added, dabbing prettily at the corner of her eye with her middle finger so that a solitary tear rolled down her cheek. She watched her father carefully from underneath her eyelashes.

"Kirsten's father took her to Rome, and Vicki's getting a dance in London and a Polo GTI," she added.

Mr. Field looked crestfallen. "Oh, sweetheart," he said, gathering her in his arms. "Of course I want you to have the very best. Forgive me—it's just been a long week, and a couple of orders were slow in coming and—forget it. You do just whatever you want and I know we'll all have a great time. OK, angel?"

Melly smiled. "Thanks, Dad," she said, beaming. Melly's smiles were always broadest when she got her own way.

"I think we must have champagne for the toast," said Mrs. Field.

"Sparkling wine?" suggested Mr. Field. "There are some very palatable Australian . . ."

"Champagne," argued his wife.

"I think," said Mr. Field wearily, popping another peppermint in his mouth, "I'll just go up to my darkroom for a bit and print up those negatives."

"All those sweets are going to make you fat," warned Mrs. Field to her husband's retreating back. "You really should resist them."

"Yes, dear," said Mr. Field.

Left to themselves, Poppy and Melissa and their mother all began talking at once about whether the cake should be sponge or fruit and how many chairs they could get into the study.

"There are enough knots here to keep a Boy Scout happy," muttered Granny Jay as she carried a tray of hot tea through from the kitchen. But everyone was far too preoccupied to hear her.

poppy gives
a helping
hand

Throughout the following week, Poppy devoted herself to bolstering Livi's ego and ensuring that Luke and Livi became an item. She had spent Saturday rooting round the stores in town trying to find something to cheer Livi up. On Monday she presented her with a smoky grey eyeshadow ("Perfect for your violet eyes," she said), a wicked lime green patent knapsack and a really cool striped T-shirt from Esprit which she knew would look great with Livi's white mini-skirt.

"But Poppy, you mustn't," protested Livi.

"Why not?" asked Poppy.

"Because it must have cost a fortune," said Livi.

"It's only money," said Poppy airily, repeating a phrase much favoured by her mother. "What's the point of having it if you don't spend it?"

Livi looked embarrassed.

"But I can't afford to get you stuff like this," she murmured. "I just don't have that kind of money."

"So?" said Poppy reasonably. "I'm not getting it because I want something back—I'm getting it because you're my friend and I like doing it."

"Thanks," said Livi.

On Tuesday, Poppy surreptitiously slipped Livi's French vocabulary book into Luke's brief-case, so that when he found it, he would have to go up to Livi and give it back. Except that halfway through break, he appeared at Poppy's arm, looking highly flushed.

"Could you give this to Livi, please?" he stammered. "It seems to have found its way into my bag." Then he spent an awful long time fiddling with his watch and asking her how things were and whether she had managed to persuade Mr. Golding to let them have a half-term disco.

Poppy, who had decided that having been

rejected on the agony column front, she should allow the dust to settle before once again attempting to drag Gee-Gee into the nineties, took heart. Luke had obviously decided that a disco would be the ideal place to chat Livi up and let everyone else see they were an item.

"I'll have a word with Gee-Gee," she said. "You'd go if there was one, wouldn't you?" she added, not wanting to waste her time unnecessarily.

"Oh, of course, yes definitely," enthused Luke.

"Great," said Poppy. "Me too." Luke looked very chuffed. She supposed he was imagining an evening of bliss with Livi. She would have to see to it.

Later that afternoon, after she had told Neil Cartwright that, yes, she could spare him two hours on Saturday to go Rollerblading and made Grant Fisher's day by agreeing to go to The Stomping Ground's Funky February disco, she approached Mr. Golding, who greeted her appearance in his study for the second time in one week with less enthusiasm than she had

81 ❖

hoped, and who said that no, they could not have a half-term disco, but that perhaps, just perhaps, he would consider allowing one on the last day of term, subject to a whole list of conditions which Poppy thought both unnecessary and unreasonable.

"I see no need," said Mr. Golding in conclusion, "for any more distractions from academic studies than is absolutely necessary. The end of term is the time for frivolity and not before."

Poppy sighed. "But sir, we do need to learn the skills of social integration," she said, praying that Gee-Gee hadn't read the *Guardian Education Supplement* the week before.

Mr. Golding made a pyramid of his hands, rested his chin on his forefingers and regarded Poppy for a moment.

"It occurs to me," he said finally, "that whatever skills you may be lacking, Poppy Field, the ability to integrate is not one of them. Good morning."

On Wednesday, Poppy had a sore throat which wasn't really that bad but in view of the fact that it was double math followed by a French test, and that she had omitted to finish her physics assignment, she decided to stay at home. Her mother, having plied her with hot lemon and rented her two videos, left for her regular mid-week game of tennis with firm instructions that she was to phone her father if she felt ill and Poppy settled herself on the settee in the sitting room and began composing her own answers to the heartrending letters in her new copy of *Sweet Talk* magazine.

She was halfway through instructions to Heidi of Sheffield concerning the matter of her warring parents when there was the sound of a key in the front door. She was just thinking that her mother's match must have been cancelled when she heard her father's voice.

"Go on through—I'll make some coffee. White with no sugar, right?"

"Lovely, thanks Leo. Oh, my goodness, Poppy . . ."

Livi's mother stood in the doorway, gaping at Poppy. This month, her hair was enlivened with purple streaks and she was wearing a bright red scarf, knotted gypsy-style under her unruly curls.

"Hi, Mrs. Hunter," said Poppy cheerily. "Mum's not here, I'm afraid—tennis," she added by way of explanation.

"I know—I mean, your father told me. Er, Leo," she called to the kitchen, "Poppy's here."

There was a clatter of coffee mugs, a muffled oath, and then Mr. Field stuck his head round the door.

"Hi, dad—I'm ill," said Poppy.

"You don't look it," said her father, handing Livi's mum a mug of coffee.

Poppy ignored this slight on the veracity of her indisposition.

"What are you doing home?" she asked.

Her father coughed. "Oh, er—I left some of the papers for Friday's meeting upstairs and Judy needs them for typing and so we came back for them."

"Oh, right," said Poppy. "By the way, Mrs. Hunter, is Livi OK?" she added.

"Fine—why shouldn't she be?" asked Judy, perching on the arm of the sofa.

"Oh nothing—I mean, I hope she hasn't

caught my sore throat," improvised Poppy, wondering how Livi's mother could be so short-sighted as to imagine her daughter was even halfway fine.

"Well, certainly she had no trouble with the vocal chords last evening," commented Mrs. Hunter. "She was on the phone for ages. I don't know what you lot find to say to one another when you are at school together all day."

Poppy opened her mouth to say that she hadn't spoken to Livi all evening and thought better of it. Perhaps Livi had got through to her dad and if she had used Poppy as an alibi, she wasn't about to blow it now.

"Some boy called Luke, I think it was," added Mrs. Hunter. "In your year, Livi said."

Yes! thought Poppy, mentally punching the air. Luke phoned Livi! Mega brill! Her plan had worked.

"He's a really nice guy, Mrs. Hunter," enthused Poppy in her most sincere manner, just to make sure that Livi's mum approached this new relationship with the right maternal atti-tude. "He really, really is."

85 ✳

"OK, I'm convinced!" grinned Livi's mum.

"I think we should be getting back to the office, Judy," said Mr. Field, casting a knowing look at Mrs. Hunter, who gulped the remains of her coffee and stood up.

It was only after her father and Mrs. Hunter had left, and she had eaten two Kit Kats in celebration of her matchmaking, and dealt, not only with Sheffield's Heidi, but with A Worried 13-year-old from Yeovil and Baffled Blur Fan from Inverness (to whom she reckoned she gave much more relevant advice on the matter of sibling relationships than *Sweet Talk*'s Cindy Lou) that Poppy stopped to wonder why it would take two people to collect one pile of papers. Then it struck her that Mrs. Hunter worked afternoons only. It was now 11:35 in the morning.

"Well?" said Poppy on Thursday morning as Livi finished Poppy's physics homework for her.

"Well what?" asked Livi.

"Luke phoned you," said Poppy.

"How do you know?" gasped Livi, looking a little pink about the gills.

"Your mum told me—she came to our house for some papers or something."

"Well, she shouldn't have," said Livi.

"Come to our house?" queried Poppy.

"Told you," snapped Livi.

This was a good sign, thought Poppy. The desire for secrecy was always very strong at the start of a relationship—she had read that in the "Talk It Over with Tessa" column of her mum's magazine.

"So—what did he want?" persisted Poppy.

"Oh, he just wanted to sort out times to practise our duet for the Three Arts Festival," she said hurriedly.

"I didn't know you were doing a duet," said Poppy.

"Well, we are now," said Livi.

"Nice one," said Poppy.

"And don't go telling everyone," warned Livi.

"Would I?" said Poppy, who assumed Livi did not yet feel ready to have her name linked with that of her new love.

"Very probably," said Livi.

poppy has a good day

Friday was Celia Field's ladies lunch day, and when Poppy arrived downstairs for breakfast she found her mother putting the finishing touches to a pile of choux puffs.

"Don't touch!" said her mother as Poppy's index finger approached the bowl of whipped cream with unerring precision.

The phone shrilled.

"Get that, Poppy, will you?" asked her mother, piping bag poised in midair.

"Leehampton 552 . . . oh, hi, Mrs. Hunter. You can't? Oh, I see. No, that's OK. I'll tell her. See you. Bye!"

Mrs Field looked expectantly at Poppy.

"That was Livi's mum—she can't come to lunch because she has to help Dad get ready for this meeting. She says sorry and everything. Can I have what she would have eaten?"

"Oh really," said Poppy's mum, ignoring her daughter's last remark. "You'd think Dad could spare her for an hour or two. I wanted to introduce Judy to Felicity Liddington—she fancies an outsize troll as an umbrella stand."

"Good grief," muttered Poppy.

"I know, darling, it's a bit bourgeois, isn't it, but then Judy needs all the work she can get," said Celia. "You know, she's not even meant to start work till two—your father really is going over the top about this meeting. I think," she added, "he's getting to be a workaholic. He hasn't had a game of golf for over two weeks."

Poppy piled three Weetabix into a bowl. "Middle-aged men who focus too much on work get stressed and run a higher risk of heart attacks," she pronounced.

"Oh thanks, I feel much better now," said her mother sarcastically.

"It's true—I read it in *Health Today*. You have to offer him relaxing diversions. It's up to the partner to take the initiative."

"I thought it would be," commented Mrs. Field dryly.

"Don't worry," said Poppy airily. "He'll come home tonight all chuffed about having signed a sales contract with some big company and be his old self again. He's only suffering the anxiety of anticipation."

Poppy's mother looked at her quizzically.

"And you, of course, would know about these things?"

"Trust me," said Poppy, and with a big grin, she snatched a choux puff from the glass dish, winked at her mother, grabbed her school bag and bounced out of the back door.

"Don't forget, we've got the afternoon off while the scholarship kids sit the exam," she called as she went. "I'm going to see Charley on the way back. Have a nice lunch. And don't worry about Dad—I'll be proved right—you'll see!"

Poppy had a very satisfying Friday morning. It started when she boarded the school bus and saw Luke and Livi sitting side by side, so deep in conversation that she had to say hello three times before they noticed her. When they did look up, they both looked very sheepish and Luke started gabbling on about some TV programme that had been on the night before. He was obviously trying to cover up for the fact that he had been chatting up Livi. It was quite clear to Poppy that her scheming was bearing fruit even faster than she could have hoped.

Mrs. Joll's PSE lesson was all about caring for others and Poppy held forth at some length about Ada and how she had disappeared just when Poppy was about to improve the quality of her life. Mrs. Joll suggested that everyone had free will and perhaps Ada had not wanted her life improved. Poppy said that was nonsense because everyone wanted a roof over their head and three square meals a day. Mrs. Joll said that maybe Poppy's idea of a solution was not the same as everyone else's, and might someone else have a chance to speak, please, but no one did, except to agree with Poppy, which was very satisfying for her and made Mrs. Joll exceedingly sulky.

At break time, Poppy's friend Tamsin, who was the best artist in the whole year but who couldn't spell to save her life, asked Poppy to help her write a letter telling Daniel Forrest to get lost, but nicely. Poppy, who saw this type of exercise as excellent practice for her agony page in the *Daily Mail*, produced what even she had to agree was little short of a masterpiece.

In history, when Mr. Ellwood was getting frightfully excited about the Boer War, Livi slipped Poppy a note.

Can you come into town tomorrow morning? It's MEGA important—I need new gear—and fast! PLEASE SAY YES!
Love xx
Livi

Poppy was convinced that the new gear was needed to wow Luke and so she nodded eagerly and spent the rest of the period ignoring the Relief of Mafeking and making a shopping list of essentials for Livi's New Look.

And just as the lunch bell went, Miss Plover

called her over and told her that two new students would be starting at Bellborough Court on the following Monday and she would like Poppy to take one of them, Tasha Reilly, under her wing.

"Tasha and Adam are twins," she explained. "Luke Cunningham is going to look out for Adam, and I am relying on you to make things easy for Tasha."

Poppy nodded eagerly. She liked to be relied upon.

Miss Plover paused and examined a thumbnail. "They haven't lived in England for some time so it will all seem a little strange, but I am sure you can help them with any problems that arise?"

"Oh yes, of course," enthused Poppy. After all, weren't problems her speciality?

conversations
at canal end

Canal End cottages, where Charley Rust and Granny Jay lived side by side in amicable enmity, were situated in a small terrace overlooking the point where the Leehampton branch of the Grand Union Canal terminated in a sheltered little backwater. In summer the area became a hive of activity for holidaymakers on their rented narrowboats, and in winter it was frequented by parties of school children who climbed over lock gates and piled into the tiny Waterways Life museum on the opposite bank to draw pictures of coal barges and aqueducts.

Granny Jay's cottage, Number 3, was immaculate, with a window box full of nodding petunias and lace curtains which ruched into symmetrical folds. Number 5, where Charley lived, was rather more battered, with paint peeling from the window frames, which rattled in the wind, and weeds pushing up through the pebbles on the path.

Poppy rang Charley's bell several times, but there was no reply. She peered in through the front window, but apart from Blisworth, Charley's cat, who was named after his favourite stretch of canal, the room was empty. She went next door to her grandmother's house.

Granny Jay opened her arms and enveloped Poppy in a lavender-fragranced hug. Her hair was bluer than ever, evidence that the previous day had been Pensioner's Day at Fringe Affairs.

"Sweetheart, what a lovely surprise!" she said. "Come on in—I've got scones just ready to come out of the oven, so you've come at the right time!"

Poppy loved her grandmother's kitchen. Granny Jay lived in the room most of the time, and in one corner was a huge armchair whose springs had long since given up, into which Poppy, having flung her school coat onto the floor, flopped with relief. At one end of the table was a huge pile of knitting—Granny Jay felt that she alone was responsible for providing balaclavas for every lifeboatman in the land. On the wall were photographs of every member of Granny Jay's family, living and dead, a selection of the results of her oil painting class and a cross-stitch sampler that read, "Today is the tomorrow you worried about yesterday, and all is well." Against the opposite wall stood an ancient cooker from which emanated the most mouth-watering smells. Poppy's mother had offered on more than one occasion to buy Granny Jay a microwave, but she had refused, saying that she didn't like the idea of radiation in her rice pudding, thank you very much.

"Well now," said Granny Jay sitting down opposite Poppy and passing her a scone, "what brings you here? Shouldn't you be in school?"

Poppy shook her head. "Half day," she said, through a mouthful of crumbs. "I came to see Charley about my project, but he's out."

"Out?" exclaimed Granny Jay with as much surprise as if Poppy had said that Charley had been spotted doing butterfly stroke in the canal.

"Now why would he want to go out?"

"For a walk?" suggested Poppy, licking butter off her fingers.

"Not at this hour," said Granny Jay decisively, glancing at her watch. "*Fifteen to One* on the telly," she added by way of explanation. She pursed her lips. "We'd best have a look," and taking a key from a hook behind the back door she beckoned to Poppy to follow her.

"I have a key because he's always locking himself out, silly old fool," said Granny Jay fondly.

They let themselves into Charley's cottage, much to the annoyance of Blisworth, who arched his back, glowered at them and leapt onto the draining board, from where he proceeded to ignore them in a most pointed manner.

A quick search revealed no sign of Charley. "His cap and his mac aren't here," said Granny Jay, inspecting the hat-stand in the tiny hallway. "He's gone out."

"That's what I said," Poppy pointed out.

"I hope he's all right," said Granny Jay, locking his front door behind her. "He's been a bit funny since all this move business came up."

"Doesn't he want to go to Victoria House?" asked Poppy. "Can't he see it makes sense?"

Granny Jay shot her a penetrating look.

"This has been his home for over fifty years," she said. "You don't just up and go without a few pangs, sense or no sense. Home is where the heart is, you know."

"I suppose so," said Poppy. "I'm glad *you've* seen sense, though, Gran—it'll be so good having you living in the garage."

Granny Jay bustled back into her own cottage and sniffed. "Yes, well, that's a maybe. There's plenty of water to flow under the bridge yet."

"But . . ." began Poppy.

"But me no buts," interrupted her grandmother briskly. "Have another scone. How's your father?"

"Fine," mumbled Poppy through a mouthful of crumbs.

"He wasn't fine last week," observed Granny Jay. "Very peaky, I thought he looked. And worried."

"Oh, he's all right," said Poppy airily. "Just in

a tizz about some stupid meeting, that's all."

"Yes, well, that's maybe a case of a blithe face on a black heart," muttered Granny Jay. Then giving herself a little shake, she said, "Oh, and I've got something for you."

She rummaged around in a drawer and produced a slightly crumpled photograph.

"That was taken back in 1953, just before the commercial barges stopped coming along here," she explained. "Coronation Year—that's why the bunting's out."

Poppy peered at the photograph. "That's Charley, isn't it?" she said, pointing to a figure on the towpath. "Who's that?"

"That," said Granny Jay proudly, leaning over Poppy's shoulder, "is your grandfather, God rest his soul. He was deputy mayor—that's him opening the museum. The real mayor had flu," she added, as if anyone who contracted a disease on such an important occasion was not to be tolerated.

"Thanks, Gran," said Poppy. "I'll put it in my project."

"That's right, love, you . . . ooh, my!" Granny

Jay stuck out her arm and grabbed blindly at the back of Poppy's chair.

"Granny? What is it—what's wrong?"

Her grandmother shook her head, rubbed her hand over her eyes, and said, "Nothing, love, nothing—just came over a bit dizzy—I'm fine now."

She flopped down on one of the wooden kitchen chairs.

Poppy looked at her anxiously. Her eyes were screwed up and her lips looked pinched and faintly blue. Poppy had never noticed it before, but suddenly it seemed that Granny Jay had grown old.

"Are you sure? Should I call the doctor?"

Granny Jay dismissed such a suggestion with an impatient waving of the hand.

"I'm as fit as a flea," she pronounced, giving herself a shake like a cat awakening from sleep and pulling her cable knit cardigan purposefully over her ample abdomen. "Just moved too fast, that's all." She glanced at the clock.

"Time you were going—you don't want to miss your bus. Do me a favour—if you see the old fool Charley on your way home, tell him to get back here. Tell him there are cheese scones baking, that'll do it."

"OK," grinned Poppy. "Are you coming for supper later?"

"Not tonight love," said Granny Jay. "That vicar's got some harebrained scheme about having a steel band at evensong—I've to sort him out."

Poppy felt quite sorry for the Reverend Wilson.

"You have to be open to change, Gran," advised Poppy. "It might be quite fun."

Granny Jay sniffed.

"Old customs are best customs," she declared. "Can't beat a nice bit of organ music. And what are you up to, then?"

"Shopping, Rollerblading, and discoing," said Poppy. "Just another run-of-the-mill weekend." As it turned out, this was one occasion when Poppy's predictions fell a little short of the mark.

She was crossing the little bridge that separated Canal End from Ecton Lane when she saw him.

101

He was sitting on a bench, throwing crumbs to a pair of overweight ducks, his shoulders hunched into his raincoat.

"Hi, Charley, I came to see you," called Poppy. "You were out," she added unnecessarily.

Charley turned and looked at her with watery blue eyes.

"Poppy—how are you, me duck?" he said, patting the seat beside him by way of invitation.

"Fine," said Poppy. "It's nice down here, isn't it?" she added, watching the ducks fighting over a piece of broken Ryvita.

Charley nodded and rubbed his chin. "Fifty-one years, I've been here. Fifty-one years." After a moment, he added, "I'll miss it."

"But Victoria House is only a couple of miles away," protested Poppy. "Gran told me," she added by way of explanation.

Charley smiled. "Oh yes, on the map it's just about that, a couple of miles. To me, it might as well be on the moon."

Poppy frowned.

Charley patted her sleeve. "See, it's like

Charley Rust, the lock-keeper, is finished. All that's left is Charley Rust, geriatric in a chair."

"Now listen, Charley," said Poppy, adopting the firm and forceful tone often used by Verity Carr, her favourite TV agony aunt. "That is a very defeatist attitude and it simply won't do, it won't do at all. You should be looking forward to this new phase—making plans, getting excited."

Charley looked at her with a wry smile.

"I should?"

Poppy nodded. "And I know the very thing," she said. "As soon as you are settled at Victoria House, you and I are going to write a book."

Charley patted her arm. "Oh, don't worry, I'll still chat to you about old times for your history doo-dah, if that's what's bothering you."

"No," said Poppy, "not that—a proper book. To be published by proper publishers and sold in the shops. It might even get made into a TV series," she added. Poppy was inclined to get carried away with her good ideas.

"I can't write no book," grumbled Charley, but Poppy noticed that he had stopped watching the ducks and was eyeing her with interest.

"You can—we can," said Poppy. "It'll be all about your life as a lock-keeper and the changes you've seen and the odd people you've met and things. And we can fill it with old pictures like this one."

She showed him the snapshot Granny Jay had given her. Charley peered short-sightedly at the picture and gave a wheezy laugh.

"Gone to seed a bit since then, haven't I, girl?" he said. "Funny you know, but inside my head I don't feel any different at all. Then I stand up and my kneecaps remind me that I am! A book, eh?" he added thoughtfully.

Poppy grinned. "Isn't it a brilliant idea! You'll become famous and get invited on to chat shows and stuff."

Charley grinned and nudged her. "I wouldn't mind sharing a sofa with that Anthea Turner," he giggled.

"Charley!" exclaimed Poppy in mock horror. "The very idea!"

Charley stood up. "Well, I'd better get back— got to keep an eye on your gran while I can.

Pretends she can do more than she can, stubborn old bat."

"She came over funny while I was there," admitted Poppy.

Charley gave her a sharp look.

"Again?" he asked.

"Has it happened before?" enquired Poppy anxiously. "But Gran's never ill."

"Thinks she's a spring chicken and goes hurtling about," Charley muttered. "I'll see to it. Don't you worry your head."

"So we'll do the book, then?" asked Poppy as Charley levered himself into a standing position.

Charley grinned. "I reckon if you say we're doing it, we're doing it—'bout as determined as your grandmother, you. And what are we going to call this book, then?" he said, crumpling the empty paper bag and stuffing it into his raincoat pocket. *"The Life and Loves of Charley S. Rust?"* He gave a wheezy chuckle.

"No," said Poppy. "I have the perfect title."

"I thought you might," said Charley. "Out with it then."

"*Rust on the Lock*," said Poppy triumphantly. "Get it?"

"Of course I get it, I'm not completely senile yet," snapped Charley. Then he grinned. "*Rust on the Lock*," he repeated. "I like it. Yes, I like it."

Charley shuffled off over the bridge, muttering, "*Rust on the Lock*," and, "I like that Anthea Turner," and Poppy headed for the bus stop, feeling exceedingly pleased with herself.

poppy gets
a shock

I f the bus hadn't had to stop at the traffic
lights, or if Poppy had been reading the
problem page in her magazine instead of
gazing out of the window and musing over the
opening paragraph of what she knew would be
her best-seller, she would never have seen
them. Which might have saved a lot of people
a lot of bother.

But as the bus ground to a halt, she glanced
into the forecourt of Henderson's car showrooms ("Quality on wheels for the discerning
driver"), and saw her father's Jaguar. Her dad
was leaning against the car with his head in
his hands and standing beside him with a
comforting arm around his shoulder was Livi's
mum.

Poppy stared. And as she watched, Judy
Hunter drew Leo's face towards hers and

kissed him very gently on the forehead. She took his hand, and led him to her silver blue Metro, and they both got in.

The last thing Poppy saw as the bus pulled away from the lights was her father running his fingers through his hair and then resting his head on Mrs. Hunter's shoulder as she manoeuvred the car out of the garage forecourt.

Poppy's heart was thumping and she felt sick. Dad and Mrs. Hunter! What was happening? What were they doing? The trouble was, Poppy knew what they were doing. She hadn't been studying problem pages in magazines for three years without realising that secret assignations in other people's cars could mean only one thing: her father was having an affair with Mrs. Hunter.

He couldn't be. Not her father. Other men had affairs—men like Mike Hunter and Hayley Spicer's dad who had gone off and married a red-head with three children that Hayley hated and despised. But her dad—he wouldn't do anything like that in a hundred years—the very idea was ridiculous. Her parents adored one another. And yet, she'd seen Mrs. Hunter kiss him, and hold his hand, and entice him into her car. She'd positively dragged him there.

That was it. It was Mrs. Hunter's fault, not her father's. She was a vamp, a man eater. Just because Livi's mum hadn't managed to hang on to her own husband, she wanted to steal someone else's. How could she? She was supposed to be her mum's best friend!

But Dad let her, she thought. And dismissed the idea at once.

Poppy got off the bus and began walking round The Crescent. Her mind was spinning. What should she do? Confront her dad? She would have to make sure her mum wasn't around, because if she guessed, it would break her heart. Should she tell Livi? That would hardly be fair, what with her worrying about her dad and . . .

That was it. Livi's dad. She had almost forgotten that she was supposed to be getting him home for Livi. Well, now she had a double reason for making sure that Mr. Hunter returned to Leehampton. It wasn't just for Livi; it was for all of them. Because if Mike Hunter came home, Mrs. Hunter would leave Poppy's dad alone.

There was no need to upset anyone. She could handle this on her own. An image of Mrs. Hunter kissing her dad swam before her eyes and for a moment, Poppy felt so angry she wanted to scream or cry. Stop that, she admonished herself firmly. This is just another problem that needs sorting calmly and quickly. Dad needed rescuing from the clutches of a devious and deserted woman. And who better to do it, thought Poppy, than his own daughter.

the plot thickens

"I can't imagine what's happened to your father," complained Poppy's mother, later that evening, as she lifted a fish pie from the oven.

He's been lured into the clutches of your so-called friend, thought Poppy miserably.

Her mother brushed a strand of hair from her face.

"Poppy, be a love and ring the office—I can't keep supper waiting any longer."

There won't be anyone there, thought Poppy, but she went into the hall and picked up the receiver.

She had just punched in the first three digits when there was a sound of car tires crunching on gravel.

"He's back!" she called out to her mother in relief and opened the front door.

CHAPTER SIXTEEN

But it wasn't her father's Jaguar that was pulling up in the driveway, but Mrs. Hunter's Metro. Her father climbed out from the passenger seat and bent down to speak to Livi's mum. Neither of them had noticed Poppy standing in the porch.

"You've got to tell her, Leo—you simply can't keep putting it off!" she heard Livi's mother insist.

"I know, you're right," replied Mr. Field. "It's just that—well, I hate to . . ."

"Do it," ordered Mrs Hunter. "Do it tonight. Delaying is only going to make matters worse."

"But Celia will be so upset . . ." began Mr. Field.

Poppy wanted to turn and run but her feet were rooted to the spot. Her mouth went dry and she was having difficulty swallowing. She could hear her heart pounding in her ears. She watched as Mrs. Hunter leaned across and took one of Leo's gloved hands in hers.

"You owe it to them, all of them," she said, gazing intently into Mr. Field's eyes. "Do it, Leo—I mean it. You have to. For everyone's sake."

Mr. Field nodded slowly.

At just that moment, Poppy's mother came to the door.

"Judy!" she called, waving a tea towel frantically as Mrs. Hunter revved the engine and reversed speedily down the driveway.

Mr. Field turned.

"Why didn't you ask Judy in?" enquired his wife. "I haven't seen her for days—she's working so hard, bless her."

Poppy couldn't bear it. She wanted to scream and say no she's not, she's seducing my father and ruining our lives. That's why she sped off as soon as she saw you. If that isn't a sign of guilt, what is? She's wicked and evil and I hate her. But she didn't say a thing.

"Where's the Jag?" asked Poppy's mother, noticing the empty space on the driveway.

Mr. Field walked wearily through to the kitchen, dumping his briefcase on the hall table.

"It's been—well, that is, I—the thing is, I had a bit of a prang," he concluded.

Poppy's mother gasped and grabbed her husband's arm.

113

"Oh no—are you hurt? Are you OK? What . . ."

Mr. Field put a reassuring arm on her shoulder.

"It was nothing—but the car will be off the road for a while, I'm afraid. Body shop job. Judy brought me home," he added.

An accident! That's why the car was at the garage. That's why Mrs. Hunter led him to her car and was making a fuss of him. He was obviously in shock.

A great flood of relief surged through Poppy's body.

"Oh, good!" she said.

"Pardon?" chorused her parents.

"I mean, oh goodness, what a lucky escape!" said Poppy. "What a good thing you weren't hurt."

So thankful was Poppy that her suspicions had been unfounded that she had two helpings of fish pie, three scoops of her mother's homemade lemon sorbet, and a large wedge of Stilton cheese. It was not until she was in bed that night suffering from a mild attack of indigestion that three thoughts struck her in quick succession. How come Mrs. Hunter was on hand when Dad had his supposed accident? What was she accusing him of constantly putting off? And worst of all, if there really had been an accident, how come that when she had seen her father's Jaguar standing in the forecourt of Henderson's showrooms, there had not been a single scratch on the paintwork?

mrs. hunter throws a spanner in the works

When the alarm shrilled on Saturday morning, Poppy had to force herself to stagger out of bed. She wasn't in the mood for shopping with Livi. She hadn't slept well; she kept dreaming that her father and Mrs. Hunter were driving across a big lake and the car began to sink. Poppy tried to rescue her dad but he kept going under the water. She woke up with a headache and a nasty niggling feeling in the pit of her stomach.

But a promise was a promise and if helping Livi to deck herself out in some wild gear would advance her romance with Luke, it was the least she could do. Besides, she had to quiz her about Mr. Hunter's movements. The one thing Poppy was determined about was that Livi's dad was going to return to the family fold, and fast.

Poppy was in the hall, zipping up her new DKNY jacket, when the front doorbell rang. It was Livi's mum.

"Hi, sweetheart!" Mrs. Hunter stepped into the hall, gave Poppy a peck on the cheek

"Mum in the kitchen?" she asked cheerfully.

Poppy glared and gave a brief nod. Seeing Livi's mum standing there as bold as brass brought everything back—the way she had held her dad's hand, the kiss, the horrible dream. And now she had the audacity to come visiting her mum as if nothing was the matter. Suddenly Poppy was glad she was going out.

"Darling, how are you?" Judy Hunter enveloped Mrs. Field in a hug and then held her at arm's length and surveyed her face anxiously. "Bearing up?"

Poppy's mother looked slightly perplexed.

"I'm fine," she said, hugging her friend. "Oh,

and thanks for driving Leo home."

Judy sat down on one of the kitchen chairs.

"It was the least I could do," she said. "How is he, poor lamb?"

Poppy glared at this overaffectionate epithet.

"I've left him to sleep," said Poppy's mum. "He was very shaken."

"Well, he would be," said Mrs Hunter. "Such an awful business."

"Yes, it was," agreed Poppy's mother, "but it could have been a lot worse."

"It could?" queried Judy.

"Well, Leo could have been badly injured," said Poppy's mother. "I mean, at the end of the day a car is just a car, isn't it—it can be mended. Or maybe we could get a new one," she added as if the thought had just struck her. "I do rather like the new Peugeot . . ."

Judy frowned.

"But Celia, how can you think about . . ." she began, and was interrupted by Poppy's father hurrying into the kitchen.

"Morning, Judy," he said cheerily, buttoning his shirt as he spoke. "Thought I heard your voice." Poppy watched as he pulled a face in Judy's direction and shook his head imperceptibly. "Talking about the accident? I had a lucky escape—pity about the car though."

Mrs. Hunter looked at Leo questioningly.

"But you . . ."

"The body shop say it will take several weeks to repair," he said and shook his head slightly once more. Something, thought Poppy, is going on between those two. And it isn't just some stupid prang with the car. Exactly what was happening, Poppy did not know. What she did know was that it made her feel very uneasy.

oh, what a tangled web we weave

"You're late," accused Livi as Poppy panted up to the doorway of Beatties department store.

"Sorry," gasped Poppy. "Bus." She didn't add that she had been so busy worrying about her father and Mrs. Hunter that she had forgotten to get off at the right stop and had had to run all the way back from the bus station. She stooped down to touch her toes in an attempt to get rid of the stitch that was crippling her side.

"Come on, quickly," urged Livi, grabbing her arm and heading for the escalator. She was wearing bright orange hipsters and a clingy bouclé top, and it occurred to Poppy that it was a long time since she had seen her look so good. It must be love.

"What are you doing?" protested Poppy. "What's the rush?"

"It's quarter to eleven," said Livi.

"So?" said Poppy.

"We were meant to be at the coffee shop five minutes ago," said Livi. "Come on."

She dragged her onto the escalator.

"Livi, will you tell me what is going on?" ordered Poppy as they reached the first floor.

"Wait and see," said Livi, breaking into a run.

The shopping mall was packed with Saturday shoppers, and they had to dodge past women with pushchairs and old ladies with trolleys. Just as they were nearing The Toasted Teacake, Livi ran full pelt past one of those little yellow triangles that say "Caution: Wet Floor," slid delicately on one foot across the diamond-patterned tiles, and landed in a rather inelegant, splayed-out position at the feet of a somewhat perplexed-looking woman wearing a lilac catsuit, which Poppy deemed to be totally inappropriate for both her age and colouring.

Poppy expected Livi to leap to her feet, utter some sort of four-letter word, and continue on her way. But she didn't. Poppy squatted down beside her and was alarmed to see that her friend's face was as white as a sheet.

Livi groaned. "My wrist," she mumbled, clutching her left hand and struggling to her knees.

"She needs to sit down," said the lilac catsuit. "Come into the café, dear."

Poppy stooped down to pick up Livi's lime green knapsack. She was just about to go inside the café and hand it back to Livi when she was struck with inspiration. She scrabbled about in the bag and found the little red address book that she had given Livi for her eleventh birthday.

"That's it!" she said, turning down a page corner. "It has to be providence!"

HUNTER, M. (Dad and wretched Rosalie)
26 Widnes Road,
Runcorn,
Cheshire
Tel: 01928-240511

She slipped the book into her pocket and went to the table where Livi was sipping a glass of water while the woman in the catsuit hovered solicitously over her. To Poppy's surprise, standing the other side of Livi, looking anxious, was Luke Cunningham.

Suddenly it all made sense. That was why Livi was so eager to get to The Toasted Teacake. Luke had asked her to meet him there and Livi wanted Poppy with her for moral support. And now, Fate had stepped in to make everything so wonderfully easy. Luke could be masterful and look after Livi and win her undying devotion and Poppy could put her new plan into action.

Luke was not looking particularly masterful, but he perked up when Poppy appeared at the table.

"Hi, Poppy, you're looking great—would you like a . . ."

"Hi, Luke—Livi, are you OK?"

Livi nodded weakly and looked at Luke.

"I'm sorry," she began. "I've spoilt . . ."

"Look," said Poppy, "I've got to dash off and do something. Luke, can you take Livi home?"

Luke looked doubtful.

"Well, actually, I was going . . ." he stammered.

"No!" A better thought crossed Poppy's mind. "I think she should go to Casualty and get an X-ray. Yes, I definitely think Casualty would be best."

"No," said Livi, "I'm fine—honestly. You and Luke should . . ."

"I must dash," said Poppy firmly. "Luke, look after her for me, won't you? I'm counting on you."

At that, Luke grinned.

"She'll be fine with me," he said, which gave Poppy great hope. Livi, however, looked exceptionally doubtful.

"Livi, don't you worry. I'll meet you at the hospital." And with an expansive wave of her hand, she left them looking after her in open-mouthed surprise.

Poppy held Livi's address book in one hand and punched in digits with the other.

"May I speak to Mr. Michael Hunter, please?

Yes, yes, I'll hold." She assumed that the squeaky voice on the other end belonged to the wretched Rosalie.

"Mike Hunter here? Who's that?"

Poppy put a handkerchief over her mouth.

"Oh Mr. Hunter, I am phoning about your daughter, Olivia." Poppy was careful to use her friend's full name. "This is the Casualty department at Leehampton General Hospital—I'm afraid your daughter has been involved in an accident."

There was a sharp intake of breath at the other end of the phone and for a moment, Poppy felt inordinately guilty. But then she reminded herself that this was all in a very good cause. Livi's happiness and the survival of Poppy's family depended on the success of her plan.

"What's happened?" Mr. Hunter's voice sounded strained.

"She fell—she collapsed in the Arndale Shopping Centre and was brought here—we think there may be a broken bone or two. The thing is, she is doing very poorly and she is asking for you."

There was silence at the other end and for a moment, Poppy thought they had been cut off. Then she heard Mr. Hunter take a deep breath and say, "Right—I'm on my way. It'll take me a couple of hours—Leehampton General, you say?"

"That's right," said Poppy.

"Is my wife with her?" enquired Mr. Hunter. Poppy thought fast.

"We were unable to reach her," she said hurriedly. "Your daughter tells me she is at a craft fair. But it's you that Olivia is asking for."

"Tell her to hang in there," said Mr. Hunter. "I'm on my way."

Two hours, thought Poppy. That should be long enough for him to be feeling really guilty by the time he gets to the hospital. Now all Poppy had to do was go to Casualty and make sure that Livi hung around looking wan until Mr. Hunter arrived.

"Olivia Hunter? No, I'm sorry, no one of that name has come in to Casualty today." The nurse looked apologetically at Poppy.

"But she must have," panted Poppy, who had run the half mile to the hospital. "I told her to. She hurt her wrist," she added.

The nurse checked her list again and shook her head.

"Sorry, dear. Perhaps your friend went home."

Poppy sighed. She had gone to all that trouble, and now Mr. Hunter would turn up and find that Livi wasn't there. She couldn't understand it—she had given them firm instructions to go straight to Casualty. Of course, it could be that they had gone home—perhaps they wanted to be alone, and with Mrs. Hunter out of the house, it would be a perfect opportunity. But what about Livi's dad? Something had to be done about that.

"I wonder if you could help me," she said to the nurse, offering her most charming and innocent smile. "You see, Olivia's father is on his way here because I . . . because he was notified of the accident. Could you tell him that his daughter is at home but asking for him constantly?"

The nurse wrote down, "O. Hunter—at home." Poppy eyed the note critically.

"You won't forget the bit about her asking for

127 ✳

him, will you?" She leaned across the desk and added confidingly, "It's a very delicate situation—she's at an emotional low."

"OK," said the nurse, whom Poppy felt was not displaying the level of concern expected of the caring profession. "Will that be all?"

"Oh, Poppy, it's you! Livi was just talking about you." Mrs. Hunter had a blob of clay on the end of her nose and wore a rather harassed expression.

Poppy hadn't expected Livi's mum to be home and she didn't really want to speak to her. She kept remembering the looks that had passed between her father and Mrs. Hunter earlier that morning. But since she was standing on the doorstep of the Hunters' house, she had little option but to talk to her.

"I came to see if Livi was all right," explained Poppy. "She wasn't at the hospital."

Livi stuck her head round the kitchen door. Poppy was a little miffed to see that the colour had returned to her cheeks and her wrist was sporting what seemed to be a particularly small and unimpressive piece of strapping.

"I'm fine," said Livi, coming to the door. "But what happened to you?"

"I, er—well," Poppy tried to come up with a plausible explanation. "I had to sort something out."

"Oh terrific, so you left Livi on her own," said Mrs. Hunter.

"But Luke was with her!" protested Poppy, who was rather disappointed that he was not there now with a comforting arm around Livi's shoulder. "He was looking after her—he's a very caring person," she added, just to increase Luke's standing in Mrs. Hunter's eyes.

"Oh yes, I suppose so," sighed Mrs. Hunter passing a hand wearily over her forehead. "I'm sorry, Poppy, forgive me—I'm really uptight at the moment."

I bet you are, thought Poppy. Don't expect any sympathy from me. Marriage wrecker.

"And I do understand that you have a lot on your mind," added Livi's mum.

Yes, like you trying to seduce my father, thought Poppy wretchedly and was just wondering what Mrs. Hunter really meant, when a blue Ford Granada with a dented front bumper screeched to a halt outside the house and Mr. Hunter leapt out.

"Dad!" cried Livi, bursting out of the front door in a manner which Poppy deemed looked far too healthy to give Mr. Hunter any ongoing cause for concern.

"Mike!" gasped Mrs. Hunter.

"Livi!" cried Mr. Hunter. "But they said you were—oh thank God! Thank God!"

"I'll be off then," said Poppy but not one of them appeared to hear her.

As she walked down the road, she turned and saw Livi enveloped in a bear hug while Mrs. Hunter looked on, flushed with what Poppy could only suppose was an onrush of passion.

She smiled serenely. That was another problem successfully solved. Now they could all get back to normal.

As it turned out, nothing was further from the truth.

problems
in the post

After the traumas of the morning, Poppy was starving when she arrived home and opened the front door expecting to be greeted with the appetising smells of lunch cooking. Instead she found her mother sitting at the kitchen table with her head in her hands and Melly pacing the floor close to tears, her normally pale skin flushed with anger.

"What's wrong?" gasped Poppy, her stomach lurching. Surely Dad hadn't told them anything about him and Mrs. Hunter—not just when Poppy had managed to get it all sorted?

Her mother looked up.

"Oh hello, darling," she said. "It's nothing, I'm sure—just a silly mix-up."

"What is?" demanded Poppy.

Melly waved a letter in the air.

"It's so humiliating!" she stormed. "I mean, how could he—how could he possibly do this to me?"

"There's probably a very simple explanation," began her mother. "I expect Dad just overlooked it, with the pressure of work and everything."

"Overlooked what? Will someone tell me what is going on?" shouted Poppy.

Melly sank into a chair and thrust the letter into Poppy's hands.

"Take a look at this!" she stormed.

"Is that all?" asked Poppy, overcome with relief that there had been no revelations about Mrs. Hunter's licentious behaviour. "It's obvious—Dad just forgot. It's easy to do."

"That's what I think," said Mrs. Field with obvious relief. "Just an oversight."

"Oh yes?" demanded Melly. "For two whole terms? He's had loads of letters—it says so."

She snatched the letter out of Poppy's hands.

"And how dare the bursar talk about making us leave school!" she cried. "It's people like us that give the school its good name."

Bellborough Court School,
Bellborough,
Northants

Dear Mr. and Mrs. Field,

Despite repeated requests for payment of the overdue school fees for Melissa and Poppy, I have still received no money since August last year.

I must therefore write to advise you that unless the unpaid amount is received in full within the next fourteen days, I will have no alternative but to consider asking you to remove your daughters from this school. In view of Melissa's imminent Advanced Level examinations, I hope that you will respond to this letter immediately and arrange an appointment at which we can discuss this most disturbing situation.

Yours sincerely,

Lawrence L. Turner

Lawrence L. Turner
Bursar, Bellborough Court

Poppy took a deep breath. She knew it would never come to that, but she was bothered about why her normally efficient father should have forgotten such an important thing as paying the fees. Probably because he has been too wrapped up in Judy Hunter to think of anything else, she thought. Perhaps she has been sucking him dry of cash. Come to think of it, she was looking a lot smarter these days. Poppy had read a lot about kept women. But it wouldn't do to voice any of these fears to her sister or mother.

"Maybe the business isn't doing so well," she suggested. "I mean, Dad did say something about things being tight? What about this meeting yesterday?"

For an instant, Poppy's mother looked anxious.

"I forgot to ask," she admitted. "You don't think . . ." Then she shook her head dismissively. "No, I'm sure it's fine. The business has always done well—your father's a very astute man. Maybe the cheque went astray. I'll have a word when he gets home from golf. Now," she added briskly, "a quick lunch and then I must get to the shops—I've still got a lot of quiches and roulades to make for the party."

Melly was not in a happy frame of mind.

"I just hope no one else finds out about this," she said to Poppy after their mother had gone shopping. "I mean, it's so demeaning—

and the bursar is really friendly with Nathan's parents."

"It's all confidential, that sort of thing," Poppy reassured her. "He wouldn't say anything. You don't think that Dad is in some sort of trouble?" she added tentatively.

"Money trouble, you mean?" asked Melly, her eyes widening in alarm. "He'd better not be— he's supposed to be getting my air ticket this week—Vicki's dad has already bought hers. And he hasn't paid for the champagne yet and they won't let us collect it till he does."

"Oh, he'll do all that," said Poppy confidently. "But I just don't understand about the school fees."

She remembered Gee-Gee's enquiry about her father being away from home. She got the feeling that the two were very much connected.

"Well, he'll have to pay them, of course," said Melly. "I just wish he hadn't been so absent-minded—I mean, we don't want to get the sort of reputation the Hunters had, do we? Remember how everyone talked when they had to sell up and move? Not that Dad is one bit like Mike Hunter, thank heavens."

Despite her sister's good intentions, mention of the Hunters did not actually make Poppy feel any better at all.

poppy faces
the music

Poppy spent the afternoon Rollerblading with Neil, an exercise which helped her forget her worries since all her concentration was focused on remaining upright. Neil seemed to take great delight in holding Poppy's hand as tightly as he could, which he assured her was purely to prevent her from falling; and he seemed unnecessarily depressed when she told him that the only way she was going to learn was to be left to do it on her own.

She had just come out of the shower, and was in her bedroom deciding whether Shimmering Sand eyeshadow was an improvement on Tawny Taupe and savouring the mouth-watering smells from her mother's party baking, when she heard a clamour at the front door. Not being one who liked to miss out on any event that might prove even mildly interesting, she put down her make-up brush and opened the bedroom door. And stopped in her tracks.

Livi's mum was standing in the hall, her hair, which now sported a saffron colour coif, spilling out of its rather haphazard French pleat, and tears streaming down her face. Poppy's mother, her chin smeared with flour, had a protective arm around her shoulders.

"He said I had played a cheap trick on him," she heard Judy sob. "He said I had got someone to phone up and pretend to be the hospital just in order to get him to come home. He said," she gulped loudly, "that I was a conniving cow."

"No!" exclaimed Poppy's mother.

"I told him I hadn't done anything, but he wouldn't believe me."

"Oh, Judy," sighed Celia, patting her on the shoulder, "I am so sorry—but surely, the hospital will confirm that they made the call?"

"That's the whole point," stressed Judy, "Mike checked and they didn't—Livi didn't even go to the hospital. She came straight home—she said Poppy was worrying unnecessarily."

"Poppy?" queried Mrs. Field. "This happened while Poppy was with Livi? She never said anything."

"Didn't she?" Mrs. Hunter sounded surprised. "She was with Livi when she fell over—but she had to dash off or something. Anyway, Luke Cunningham brought Livi home. What I want to know is who could have phoned Mike?" She paused. "He believes it was me because not many people know his number. Now he's stormed off back to Rosalie—and Livi's in pieces and . . ."

"Come and have a cup of tea," said Celia soothingly, and at that point, the kitchen door closed and all Poppy could hear was the murmur of voices and the clatter of the cake tin.

Poppy sank down on her bed feeling uncomfortably guilty. It wasn't meant to be working out like this. Mr. Hunter was meant to have realised just how much he missed Livi and Judy and being at home; he should have been out celebrating their reunion, not dashing up the motorway to Runcorn. If only Livi had gone to the hospital as Poppy had planned; if Mr. Hunter had seen her lying white and wan on a trolley looking all pathetic his heart would have softened, she knew it would. Why couldn't Livi have done as she was told? Why didn't Luke carry out her instructions? It was one thing to help people in a crisis and quite another when they blew your plans through their own stupidity and lack of foresight.

And now to make matters worse, Mrs. Hunter was weeping all over Mum, who was probably being as nice as pie without realising that she was consoling the very woman who was plotting to steal her husband. Judy might pretend to be bereft at the loss of Mike, but she was probably the sort of woman who collected men like some people collected postage stamps.

Despite all the arguing she was conducting in her head, she couldn't forget Mrs. Hunter's last remark. "Livi's in pieces." Poppy nibbled on her knuckles. Had she made things worse? She'd wanted to make Livi happy, not even more miserable than she was.

"Poppy!" Her thoughts were interrupted by her mother's insistent call. "Poppy, will you come down here please!" It was very definitely an order and not a request.

Poppy took a deep breath. She knew that the next ten minutes were going to be rather uncomfortable.

"But, Poppy, can't you see that it was none of your business?" asked Judy Hunter after the whole story had been told three times over. "What possessed you to interfere?"

Poppy sighed. "Livi was miserable," she said. "She kept on about how much she missed her dad, and how it was impossible to talk to you about it and I thought that if I could make him come home, he'd realise how much nicer you were than Rosalie." Poppy bit her lip to stop herself from crying. "It's all a matter of communication, you see," she added knowledgeably.

"Oh is it?" snapped Judy. "Well, it hasn't helped. What do you mean, Livi couldn't talk to me?" she added anxiously.

"She said that you got irritated when she mentioned her dad and then she felt guilty for wanting him back when you didn't."

Judy shook her head and smiled ruefully. "Oh, I want him back all right and I know how much

Livi wants him too—which is why I had to leave things to take their course and not push it. That's the way it works with Mike."

If she wants Mr. Hunter back, thought Poppy, perhaps she doesn't want Dad after all. This was a good sign.

"I'm sorry," said Poppy. "It's just that when Livi fell over and I found her address book, it all seemed like Fate. I didn't mean to mess things up, honestly."

Judy reached over the table and laid her hand on Poppy's. Poppy noticed distractedly that there were little bits of clay under every one of her fingernails.

"Oh, Poppy," she sighed. "I'm sure you meant well, but you only know half the story. You see, I knew full well that if I left Mike to his own devices he'd be home within a month or two. He always is—that's his way. He has his little fling, convinces himself he is still desirable—whatever that means," she added with a sigh, "and then he comes home with his tail between his legs and life jogs along for a while longer."

Poppy stared at her. "But that's not the right way to go about it," she exclaimed. "That's crazy!"

"Poppy!" cried her mother. "Apologise to Mrs. Hunter this minute!"

Livi's mum held up a hand.

"It's all right, Celia," she said. "Poppy has a point. It's certainly not what the feminists would have me do, is it? But you see, Poppy, the point is, it works for me. Just as going off to my retreats helps me get through it—oh, yes, I know you have a laugh, Celia," she grinned at her friend. Celia smiled ruefully back.

"The thing is, now Mike will feel he has to make a point, and he will stay away even longer," sighed Judy.

"I'm sorry," whispered Poppy.

"I know you are," said Judy. "But just remember, while caring about people and trying to help them is a wonderful thing, taking over their lives is something altogether more dangerous."

Poppy nodded.

"Do you think Livi will forgive me when she finds out?" she asked.

"We'd better go and ask her, hadn't we?" suggested Mrs. Hunter. "The car's outside."

Poppy was about to protest that Grant was picking her up in an hour but thought better of it. Making things right with Livi was rather more important than an evening at The Stomping Ground.

break
friends,
make
friends

CHAPTER TWENTY-ONE

"She's in her room, you had better go up," said Mrs. Hunter.

Poppy knocked on Livi's door and walked in.

Livi was sitting on her bed staring out at the rain. She turned round as the door opened, and Poppy saw that she had been crying.

"Hi, Livi," she said nervously. "I've got something for you."

She put her hand in her jacket pocket and handed Livi her address book.

Livi tried one of those overbright smiles that people try when they want to look as though nothing is the matter.

"Oh, thanks, I must have dropped it when I . . ." She stopped. The corner of the page with all the Hs was turned down. Slowly Livi raised her eyes and looked at Poppy.

"It was you," she whispered, "you phoned my dad. Does my mum know?"

Poppy nodded. "I thought that . . ." she began.

"No, you didn't!" shouted Livi, jumping off the bed. "You didn't think at all. My dad has had a blazing row with my mum and called her all sorts of horrid names and made her cry, and now he's gone back to Rosalie and it's all because of you. You think you're so clever, don't you? Well, you're not! You don't know anything! I hate you Poppy Field, I hate you!"

Poppy was close to tears. "But you said you wanted me to come up with a plan," she protested. "And when you fell over and I found the book, it seemed like a brilliant idea."

Livi rounded on her. "Oh yes, and you didn't think to tell me about it, did you? You just bulldozed off and did your own thing and didn't give a toss what happened as a result! You've just made everything worse!"

Poppy felt terrible. It was true; if Mr. Hunter had gone for good, Livi's mum would try to get her claws into Dad. And to make it worse, Livi had turned against her and everything was falling apart.

"I only did what I did because I wanted you to be happy," she said. "You wanted to see your dad and . . ."

Livi burst into tears. "Yes, but I wanted him to come because *he wanted to* not because someone made him feel he had to and told him lies to get him here. If he loved me, he wouldn't have to be told!"

She turned away, clamping her hand over her mouth, and stared out of the window.

Poppy put an arm around her shoulder. "He does love you, I know he does," she said softly. "It's my fault this has all gone wrong, but I will put it right, I promise."

Livi shrugged her arm away.

"Don't bother," she snapped. "You've done enough damage already."

Poppy moved away.

"I'm sorry," she whispered.

"It's not just me," said Livi. "My mum was really upset, what with being so worried about your dad and . . ."

She stopped and looked flustered.

Poppy felt sick. So Livi knew too.

"What about my dad?" she snapped, her stomach churning.

Livi turned away.

"Nothing," she muttered.

Poppy gave up trying to be controlled and burst into tears.

"Yes, well I'm as keen on your dad coming home as you are, because then your mother might leave my dad alone!" she shouted.

"What are you talking about?" asked Livi.

"Your mum," said Poppy through strangled sobs, "is having an affair with my father."

"Oh don't be so stupid!" protested Livi. "My mum doesn't do things like that, and anyway, she adores my dad—she's told me so heaps of times."

Now it was Poppy's turn to get irate.

"Oh yes?" she cried. "So why does she keep holding my dad's hand, and kissing him and telling him that he must come clean with my mum? Tell me that!"

Livi bit her lip and looked puzzled.

"I don't know," she said. "I suppose she's just trying to be nice to him, what with the business and everything."

Poppy stared at her.

"What do you mean?"

"Look," said Livi, "I'm not supposed to say anything, but my mum said your dad is having trouble with the company and she will probably lose her job."

Poppy didn't say a word. She sat on the end of Livi's bed and thought about how her dad said money was tight, and about the unpaid school fees and Dad's reluctance to talk about holidays. She thought abut his outburst over Melly's party plans and how he always looked anxious and forlorn these days. Could it be that she had got it all wrong? But she never got things wrong. Did she?

She swallowed and a big tear trickled down her cheek.

Livi took her hand.

"I'm sorry—Mum said I wasn't to mention a

149 ⁂

thing until he'd told you himself—she's been try-ing to persuade him to say something for days."

Poppy shook her head and wiped her eyes.

"It's OK," she said. "I'm glad I know. At least now I can do something about it. There must be a solution."

Livi raised her eyebrows in mock despair. "If there is, Poppy Field is bound to be the one to find it," she said.

Poppy smiled a watery smile.

"Friends?" she said tentatively.

"Friends!" asserted Livi and gave her a big hug.

"I needed that," smiled Poppy.

"Me too," said Livi.

Poppy was so relieved that they were friends again that she forgot to ask Livi just how Luke had professed his undying love for her.

mrs. hunter tells it how it is

"**M**rs. Hunter, I know about Dad's business," said Poppy as she and Livi demolished a packet of chocolate digestive biscuits at the breakfast bar.

Judy looked up in surprise from painting an angry-looking little gnome.

"I thought maybe he hadn't said anything—this morning, when I . . ."

Poppy shook her head.

"No, he hasn't," she said. "Livi told me."

Judy rounded on her daughter.

"Livi, you promised . . ."

"It slipped out—sorry," confessed Livi.

Mrs. Hunter glared at her.

"It wasn't her fault," insisted Poppy. "You

see, I thought you were having a secret affair with Dad and she told me you weren't and . . ."

Judy dropped her paintbrush in amazement.

"You thought *what*?"

Poppy took a deep breath. "When you brought Dad home after the accident, you were holding his hand and telling him to speak to Mum, and I'd already seen you kissing him on the forecourt of Hendersons and driving him off in your car and . . ." To her extreme embarrassment, Poppy felt tears welling up in her eyes. She shook herself. "Anyway, that's what I thought."

Mrs. Hunter jumped up and put a paint-spattered arm round Poppy.

"Oh Poppy, I'm so sorry," she exclaimed. "Surely you know me better than that—I wouldn't do such a thing."

Poppy looked unconvinced.

"Look, love, I'd better tell you," said Mrs. Hunter. "There was no accident. Your father's car was leased from Hendersons, and he didn't—he had difficulty keeping up with the repayments and so they repossessed it. He had to take it back to the garage and I just followed him in my car in order to drive him home."

Poppy frowned.

"But you kissed him," she insisted.

Mrs. Hunter smiled ruefully.

"Did I? Yes, I probably did give him a friendly kiss—he's so upset about everything, you know. But that's all it was—a friendly peck. No more."

Poppy stared at her.

"And as for encouraging him to talk to your mum—well, of course I did. She has to know— you all had to know—sooner or later."

"How bad is it?" whispered Poppy.

Judy sighed.

"It's not really for me to say, love—I've probably said far too much already. After all, at the end of the day it is none of my business. The best thing would be for you to talk to your dad about it all," she suggested.

Poppy looked her straight in the eye.

"It's not just a little hiccup, is it?" she said.

Mrs. Hunter took a deep breath.

"No, Poppy," she said. "I am rather afraid it isn't."

poppy plays the good samaritan

Poppy refused Mrs. Hunter's offer of a lift home. She needed time alone to think. She phoned Grant from a phone box and invented a migraine and then spent ten minutes persuading him not to come round to the house and offer her solace.

As she walked down Ecton Lane to The Crescent, thoughts crowded into her mind until she couldn't think straight. Why hadn't Dad told them about the business? Why had he told a lie about having an accident? Was it all really so bad that he couldn't bring himself to talk about it?

Poppy felt a tight little knot forming in the pit of her stomach. She thought about all the times her mum had bought new clothes and shoes and giggled about the price and thrown away the receipts. She remembered how Melly had chattered on about champagne and discos and how weary and anxious her father had looked. And she remembered Granny Jay saying that dad was putting "a blithe face on a black heart." Had she guessed that something was wrong?

I should have realised too, thought Poppy. After all, I'm supposed to be good at that sort of thing. But then, she had never expected to find problems on her own doorstep; they always seemed to be things that happened to other people.

Except that now, if what Mrs. Hunter said was true, they did have a problem.

A big one. And it was up to Poppy to get her dad to tell them the truth, the whole truth and nothing but the truth. And then she would simply have to work out ways of putting everything to rights.

As she rounded the corner by the primary school, Poppy saw Ada. She was dressed just as she had been before, except that the feather in her hat had been replaced by a bright yellow daffodil. She was leaning with her elbows on the school wall and her chin resting on her hands.

"Hi, Ada," said Poppy tapping her lightly on the shoulder.

Ada shot round, a frightened look in her eye. And Poppy gasped.

Across Ada's rather wrinkled forehead was a large cut. A thin trickle of blood ran over the bridge of her nose.

"Ada!" gasped Poppy. "What happened?"

"A slight contretemps with two louts who felt I should not be sitting where they wanted to sit," said Ada with just the slightest tremble in her voice. "It's nothing—just a minor inconvenience."

Poppy took charge.

"You're coming back to my house," she said firmly, taking Ada's arm and leading her across the road. "You need a plaster on that and a cup of hot, sweet tea." (Poppy was a keen viewer of medical dramas on television.)

Somewhat to Poppy's surprise, Ada made no objection.

When they reached Poppy's house, Mr. Field was in the kitchen adding up columns of figures in a red cash book. As Poppy barged through the back door, he slammed the book closed and looked up rather furtively.

"Dad, this is Ada—she's been assaulted," said Poppy dramatically. Mr. Field looked suitably alarmed.

"My dear lady," he said, jumping up and pulling out a chair for Ada. "What happened?"

"Your daughter is prone to exaggeration," smiled Ada and related the story of her injury. "Not many people refer to me as a lady," she added softly.

"My wife is out, I'm afraid," explained Poppy's father. "Granny Jay's had another funny turn," he said to Poppy by way of explanation.

Poppy frowned. She was getting worried about her grandmother. The sooner the garage was converted, and they could keep a close eye on her, the better it would be.

"Poppy, run upstairs and get the plasters, and some antiseptic," instructed her father. "Now, Mrs. . . ."

"Featherstone, Ada Featherstone," said Ada, clasping Leo's proffered hand.

"Tea, Mrs. Featherstone?"

"How kind," said Ada. "Do you have Earl Grey?"

When Poppy returned to the kitchen, clutching the entire contents of the medicine cabinet, she found her father and Ada engaged in animated conversation over a pot of tea and a plate of the raisin and oatmeal biscuits which her mother usually reserved for visiting vicars and members of the tennis team.

"How very, very interesting!" Mr. Field was gazing intently at Ada's weather-beaten face.

Poppy dabbed at Ada's cut with some damp cotton wool and wondered whether perhaps she should be a nurse rather than an agony aunt.

"Ada tells me you know one another," said her father.

Ada grinned.

"Oh indeed we do," said Ada. "Your daughter was kind enough to furnish me with a couple of fashion accessories a few days back." She winked at Poppy.

"Mrs. Featherstone has most kindly agreed to allow me to take some photographs of her," said Poppy's father. "I think she would be a perfect subject for the *Faces of Our Age* competition in *The Sunday Times*." Poppy noticed that her father appeared more animated and eager than he had been for days. Perhaps Mrs. Hunter had got it all wrong and whatever problems there had been had all been put to rights.

"So if I may—tomorrow, around two o'clock?" asked Mr. Field politely. "Down by the canal, I think, near the lock gates? The light should be just right then."

"I'll be there," affirmed Ada.

"You don't have to go," declared Poppy. "You can sleep in the spare room."

Ada shook her head.

"Thank you, but no," she said. "I am meeting a friend for a little light supper and a chat." She made it sound as if they were dining at the Ritz. "I can't let her down at this late stage."

She turned to Poppy's father.

"Until tomorrow, then," she said.

"Of course," said Poppy's father, "I shall make it worth your while."

Ada pulled herself to her full height and shook her head.

"Oh no," she said sternly. "What I do I do because I want to. For no other reason. However," she added hesitantly.

"Yes?" murmured Mr. Field.

"A copy of the daily newspaper would be much appreciated. With the crossword untouched," she added firmly. "And I am mighty partial to bananas."

Mr. Field grinned and Poppy realised how long it was since she had seen her dad look cheerful.

"Of course," he said. "I shall remember."

poppy does some plain speaking

"**S**uch an interesting woman!" said Mr. Field after Ada had left. "That face— so expressive; she will make a wonderful subject. I think a little back lighting . . ."

"I wish you had insisted that she stayed the night," said Poppy in an accusing manner. "She'll probably be sleeping in some grotty barn."

Mr. Field shook his head. "I rather feel that she wouldn't want that," he said. "She's a woman who likes her independence. You have to respect that. And besides," he added dryly, "I hardly think Mum would see Ada as a desirable house guest."

At the mention of her mother's name, the knot returned to Poppy's stomach.

"Dad?" she began.

"Yes?"

"Why didn't you tell us that the business is in trouble?"

There was a sharp intake of breath from her father who stopped dead in his tracks and turned to face her.

"Who told you that?" he blustered. "There's no real problem—just a minor hiccup, a little bit of a cash flow problem, nothing that . . ."

"DAD!" shouted Poppy. "This is me. Poppy. Your daughter. Don't lie to me. Tell me to mind my own business. Tell me I won't understand if you must. But don't ever, ever lie to me!"

Her father closed his eyes and swallowed.

"I'm sorry, sweetheart," he said softly. "Who told you?"

"Mrs. Hunter," said Poppy. Her father opened his mouth to speak. "And before you say anything, she only did it because I told Livi that I thought you and she were having a rip roaring affair."

Mr. Field looked at her incredulously.

"What?" he stuttered.

"I saw you together and she was holding your hand and telling you that you had to come clean and I thought . . ."

Mr. Field put a hand on her shoulder.

"Oh, Poppy, Poppy. Nothing could be further from the truth. Judy's been a tower of strength—but an affair? No way. Honestly," he added, a pleading tone in his voice.

"I believe you," said Poppy. "But why didn't you tell us you were in trouble?"

"Oh, I wouldn't call it trouble exactly," began her father, unwrapping a mint and slipping it into his mouth.

"DAD! Honesty, remember. Judy said the Jag had been repossessed."

Leo closed his eyes and bit his lip.

"Oh," he said.

"And we all know that you haven't been paying the school fees—a letter came. Melly wasn't very happy," she added.

Her father's shoulders sagged and he suddenly seemed smaller and older. "Ah. Well, I suppose I had better go to the school on Monday and sort that out. If I can," he added under his breath.

Poppy looked alarmed.

"It will be OK in the end, won't it, Dad?" she asked.

Her father straightened his shoulders, put an arm round her waist and hugged her to him.

"'Course it will, sweetheart," he said reassuringly. "Things aren't going wonderfully just now, so I had to give up the car, but I've a couple of bright ideas up my sleeve and with a bit of luck, I'm sure I can sort it out. It's nothing for you to worry your head about."

"And you'll tell Mum and Melly? Tonight?" pleaded Poppy.

"No," said her father, so firmly that Poppy didn't argue. "Melly's party is next Saturday and we are all going to have a great time. I owe her that much at least," he added.

"But . . ." began Poppy.

"Promise me you won't mention this conversation to your mum or Melly?" asked her father. "I'll tell you all everything next Sunday after the party—but by then, it will probably all be sorted and everything will be back on an even keel. No point worrying them if there's no need, is there?

Best wait, don't you think?"

"OK," said Poppy reluctantly.

"Don't look so worried," encouraged her father. "It'll all be fine, you'll see."

Poppy knew he meant to make her feel confident. But somehow, it wasn't working.

poppy falls
in love

I t wasn't until Poppy was unpacking her school bag into her locker on Monday morning that she remembered that she was supposed to be looking out for the new girl, Tasha Reilly. She had been so preoccupied with worries about her father and an enormous urge to spill the beans to her mum, who had spent all breakfast trying to get Poppy to tell her whether to buy a Louis Feraud suit or a Donna Karan dress for Melissa's party, that she had forgotten all about it being Tasha's first day.

She was scanning the yard for someone who looked lost when she felt a tap on her shoulder.

"Can you tell me where Luke Cunningham hangs out?"

Poppy looked over her shoulder. And stared. Standing beside her was the most divinely gorgeous boy she had ever seen. He had dancing indigo-coloured eyes, skin the colour of milky coffee, and dark, wavy hair that just begged to have fingers run through it. He grinned at Poppy, and as she gazed mesmerised into his face, all the worries that had crowded her mind minutes before disappeared, to be replaced by one, overriding thought—that whoever this drop-dead delicious guy turned out to be, she was not going to let him out of her sight.

"Luke Cunningham?" repeated the boy, as Poppy remained dumbstruck.

"Oh, yes, sorry," she said hastily. "He's in my year—I'll take you. I'm Poppy Field," she added.

"Adam Reilly," said the vision. "It's my first day—we've just moved to Leehampton."

"Oh, then it's your sister I'm supposed to be looking after," said Poppy. "Is she around?"

"Over there, talking to that fair-haired girl."

Poppy glanced and saw Livi chatting to a tiny, olive-skinned girl with a mop of dark curly hair and a rather worried expression. She switched her gaze back to Adam and thought what wonderful eyes he had.

"I think she's a bit nervous about starting here," said Adam. "It's all so different from where we used to live."

"I'll take care of her," Poppy reassured him. "She'll be fine with me."

"I'm sure she will." Adam grinned at her and a little shiver galloped down Poppy's spine. "Thanks," he added.

At that moment Luke dashed up, hair awry and spectacles askew.

He grinned at Poppy. "Hi," he said. And grinned again.

"Hi, Luke, this is Adam—you are supposed to be looking out for him," said Poppy.

"Oh, right. Sorry—I got tied up," said Luke. "You'd better come with me—it's Registration in five minutes."

"Thanks for your help, Poppy," said Adam with a smile that had a simultaneous and rather dramatic effect on Poppy's heart rate and ability to stand. "See you around?"

"Oh yes," breathed Poppy. You bet, she added silently.

* * *

"Your brother's nice, isn't he?" said Poppy casually as she shepherded Tasha to registration.

"He's OK," said Tasha noncommittally.

"Has he got a girlfriend?" asked Poppy.

Tasha smiled shyly.

"Not one," she said. Poppy's heart soared.

"Dozens," added Tasha with a giggle.

Poppy's heart plummeted.

"But he left them all behind when we moved," said Tasha.

Poppy's heart rallied.

"Why?" said Tasha. "Do you fancy him?"

"This is where we have Registration," said Poppy, neatly evading the issue. She had never felt like this before. But if a dry mouth, galloping heart rate, undisciplined knees, and a total inability to think of anything but that mind-blowing smile and undoubtedly kissable lips were signs of fancying someone, then she could only suppose she did.

In the middle of a particularly boring geography lesson, during which Miss Plover had got very excited over a video on the effects of acid rain, and Poppy had developed a crick in the neck from constantly looking over her shoulder at the wall chart of the Himalayas so that she could check out Adam, Livi rattled her ruler to attract Poppy's attention and slipped her a note.

Isn't Adam gorgeous? Seeing him has made me realise you were right—Ben was never the one for me. It's Adam. And I think he likes me—he keeps looking this way and smiling. You will have to tell me what to do to make him ask me out. I'm relying on you to come up with a foolproof scheme.

Love, Livi ♡

Poppy screwed up the note and threw it into her school bag. No way was she about to help Livi get it together with Adam. After all, how would poor Luke feel? Livi couldn't just ditch him like that. And besides, Livi wasn't right for Adam. Poppy guessed he needed a spunky, go-getter girlfriend, someone who wasn't afraid to speak her mind and get things done. Someone, in fact, just like Poppy.

* * *

After lunch, while Tasha was having what Miss McConnell called an orientation session, which actually involved being told what you were not allowed to do and when you couldn't do it, Livi cornered Poppy outside the locker room.

"So what do I do?" she said, flicking her hair behind her ears.

"About what?" said Poppy.

"About Adam, of course!" said Livi. "He is just so gorgeous! What do I have to do to get him to go out with me?"

"Nothing," said Poppy emphatically.

"What do you mean, nothing?" objected Livi.

"Remember what I told you? You have to be elusive and mysterious—let him think he has to fight for your attention. It's no good coming on strong, that's a sure turnoff," she added.

"You really think so?" said Livi doubtfully.

"Trust me," said Poppy.

And if she felt just the tiniest niggle of conscience, she assured herself that it was all for Livi's own good. She should stick with Luke. And leave Adam to Poppy.

poppy lays the bait

Throughout the week, Poppy did all she could to attract Adam's attention. She took to getting up half an hour early in order to wash her hair and apply her eyeliner with minute precision. She discovered that Adam was trying out for the squash team and stayed late to watch him practise. At lunch time, she made sure that she and Tasha sat on the same table as Adam, using the excuse that Luke and Livi had to practise their duet for the Three Arts Festival and Adam mustn't be allowed to feel abandoned.

By Thursday, she was getting worried. Adam was very friendly and chatty, but he hadn't asked her out and if she was honest, he was just as nice to everyone else as he was to her. When she tried to be sparklingly witty, it was Luke who laughed loudest at her jokes and when she said she had left her lunch money in her locker, it was Luke who leapt from his seat to fetch it. Adam just carried on eating.

"So where are all the happening haunts in Leehampton, then?" asked Adam as they waited for the school bus.

"The Stomping Ground's the best," said Livi. "I'll take you there one night if you like."

Poppy glared at her and raised her eyebrows. So much for being mysterious and elusive.

"Brilliant!" said Adam. "How about tomorrow night?"

"Can't," said Livi, reluctantly. "It's Melissa's—that's Poppy's sister—it's her eighteenth birthday bash."

"To which," said Poppy hastily, with as charming a smile on her face as she could muster, "you are invited—and you, too, Luke."

"Mega!" said Luke, beaming broadly.

"No," said Tasha. "Thanks, anyway."

"Pardon?" said Poppy.

"I don't like parties much," said Tasha shyly.

"You'll like this one," said Poppy. She wasn't

risking Adam staying away for the sake of his sister.

Tasha looked highly doubtful.

"Come on, Tasha, give it a go," said Adam. "I'll be there, and you know Luke and Livi."

Poppy held her breath.

"OK," said Tasha.

"Great," said her brother. "It'll give us a chance to get to know some other people."

Never mind the other people, thought Poppy. All I am concerned with is making sure you get to know me. Really, really well.

party
predicaments

On the morning of Melly's birthday, everyone gathered around the breakfast table.

"Happy birthday, Melly darling!" Mrs. Field enveloped her elder daughter in a hug and presented her with an exquisitely wrapped package topped with a gold and silver bow.

It was a state-of-the-art camera, with built-in zoom lens and idiot-proof focusing.

"That's wicked, Mum!" gasped Melly. "It must have cost a fortune."

Mrs. Field looked pleased.

"It was recommended in your father's photography magazine," she said. "And I did want you to have the very best."

Mr. Field looked slightly sick.

"And this is from me," said Poppy. Melly ripped off the paper and found a hand-marbled, loose-leaf book with the words "Traveller's Journal" embossed on the front and a tiny gold ballpoint pen.

"So you can keep a record of all you do and then write a best-selling travel book," explained Poppy.

Melissa hugged her.

"It's brilliant, Poppy—thanks!"

Mrs. Field fingered the book appreciatively.

"What a lovely idea—isn't it, Leo?" she said.

Poppy's father smiled a rather forced smile.

"And this," said Granny Jay, fishing into her capacious handbag, "is a little bitty something from me."

"Gran!" gasped Melly. "You shouldn't have."

In a tiny, velvet-lined box, were a pair of double pearl earrings.

"My mother gave those to me on my twenty-first," explained Granny Jay. "Take care of them."

"I will, Gran, I will," said Melissa, hugging her. "They are beautiful."

"Now give her the ticket, Leo darling," gushed Mrs. Field impatiently.

"Ah, well," began Mr. Field, studying the daisy chain motif on the tablecloth in some considerable detail, "there is just the smallest hiccup over that."

Melly's face fell.

"Hasn't come through yet," he gabbled. "Typical, isn't it? Still, you're not leaving today, are you?"

Melly looked resigned.

"But it will come soon, won't it?" she asked.

Leo made a coughing noise in his throat and jumped up from the table.

"Well, I'd better go and put those flares up the drive ready for tonight," he said and disappeared into the garden.

Poppy gave a little twirl in the mirror. She was wearing a scarlet dress with spaghetti straps and a pair of the funkiest black and perspex PVC mules which *Yell!* magazine had said were the must-have footwear of the decade. She had braided the top of her hair and let the rest fall loose and spent ages making up her eyes to look sultry yet demure. She was very pleased with the result.

At that moment, the doorbell rang and she heard Melissa greeting the first of her guests. Blowing a kiss at her reflection in the mirror, she took a deep breath and prepared to sweep Adam off his feet.

It turned out to be rather more difficult than Poppy had hoped. Adam appeared to be spending an inordinate amount of time with Livi and to make matters worse, Luke didn't seem the slightest bit put out. He asked Poppy to dance and didn't look over his shoulder at Livi once the whole time, but chatted away with more animation than Poppy had ever thought him capable of.

"You look gorgeous," he breathed, pulling her towards him.

"Thanks," said Poppy, watching out of the corner of her eye as Adam and Livi started to dance.

"I really like you a lot, you know," said Luke.

"Mmm," said Poppy, thinking that it was totally unnecessary for Livi to clasp Adam quite that tightly.

"You do? Really?" said Luke.

"Pardon? Oh yes, yes," said Poppy wondering what on earth he was going on about.

When Poppy saw Adam tenderly remove a flick of hair from Livi's left eye and stroke her forehead, she thought she would explode with jealousy. What was Livi thinking of? She already had a boyfriend.

Adam leaned towards Livi and appeared to be perilously close to kissing her on the lips, when Mrs. Field flicked all the lights on and entered the room bearing a huge birthday cake.

"Now, everyone, Melly is going to cut her cake," she announced. Melly, flanked by Jake and Nathan who were each trying to look as if the other wasn't there, gasped in delight at the cake. In one corner was a map of Great Britain and in the opposite corner, a map of Australia. Linking the two were the words:

HAPPY BIRTHDAY AND HAPPY TRAVELLING TO MELISSA ANNABEL JANE

Everyone gathered round and oohed and aahed appreciatively and said things like, "You're so lucky going to Australia, Melly," and, "I wish my parents were that cool!" and, "Make a wish," and Melly cut the cake and everyone sang Happy Birthday and clapped. Nathan swept Melissa into a passionate embrace and everyone clapped again, and then Jake hugged her and kissed her nose. It was only because Poppy was busily scanning the room to find out where Livi and Adam had got to that she noticed her father silently slipping out of the conservatory door. He didn't look like someone who was enjoying a good party. He looked like a man with the cares of all the world on his shoulders.

Partly because she was feeling miffed at Livi and partly because she wanted to do something to get rid of the knotted feeling in the pit of her stomach that seemed to hit her these days whenever she thought about her dad, Poppy sashayed up to Adam, grabbed his arm playfully and dragged him on to the disco floor.

"Come on, let's see how you dance!" she teased.

For the next fifteen minutes they danced and talked about everything under the sun. Adam told Poppy how homesick he and Tasha were for Singapore, where they had lived since they were tiny, and how Tasha hated the cold and he hated the damp and how hard it was leaving their friends behind. The more he talked, the closer they danced and Adam was just starting to do rather exciting things with Poppy's ear lobes, when he pulled away, looking guilty.

"We'd better stop," he said.

"Why?" said Poppy, grabbing his wrists and starting to dance again.

"Well, Luke's been a really good mate to me and what with you being his girlfriend and everything . . ."

Poppy roared with laughter and shook her head.

"No way!" she said. "Luke and Livi are an item, not . . ."

Adam stared at her wide-eyed.

"But Livi told me that Luke is besotted with you and that she was the one who got you two together in the first place," he said.

"She did *what?*" exclaimed Poppy.

Adam looked rather sheepish.

"The other day I told Livi I thought you were cute . . ."

"You do?" breathed Poppy.

" . . . and she said, bad luck because she's already spoken for. So I backed off," he muttered.

"But that's ludicrous!" expostulated Poppy. "I was the one who got Luke and Livi together."

"Excuse me?" Adam looked confused. "But Luke's forever saying how amazing you are."

"Never mind all that—go and dance with your sister," ordered Poppy, gesturing towards the corner of the room where Tasha was sitting looking rather lost. "I'll be back."

"If that's your idea of revenge, then I think it's a pretty cheap one!" shouted Poppy.

She had dragged Livi away from the party and upstairs to her bedroom.

"What are you on about?" asked Livi.

"Telling Adam that Luke and I are a couple," said Poppy. "Just because you suddenly want to be rid of poor Luke and get your claws into Adam, there's no need to make up stories about him and me fancying each other."

"What do you mean, I want to be rid of Luke? I was never with Luke, so how can I . . . ?"

"Don't give me that!" ranted Poppy. "I've seen you in huddles with him and then that Saturday when you two had arranged to meet and you wanted me for moral support . . ." began Poppy.

Livi stared at her. "Luke had asked me to get you there so he could be with you—then I was supposed to disappear off shopping and he was going to ask you to go to the cinema or something." She sighed. "Only then I fell over and it all went wrong."

Poppy frowned.

"You mean, you set me up?" she demanded. "How dare you try to organise my life?"

"Oh, that's rich, coming from you!" snapped Livi. "What do you think you spend your time doing?"

"That's different," said Poppy. "I mean, I had worked it so that you and Luke could get it together, then you would forget that jerk Ben and be happy again. Luke is just right for you, Livi."

Livi glared at her.

"No, he is not!" she said. "Just because you think it would be a neat idea doesn't mean it can work. I don't fancy Luke; Luke doesn't fancy me. Luke fancies you something rotten. End of story."

"And you fancy Adam?" asked Poppy, heart in her mouth.

"Yes, I do," affirmed Livi.

"Well, you should play hard to get," ordered Poppy.

"Oh yes," said Livi sarcastically, "just like you've been doing all evening? Well, this time I am going to play it my way. And now if you have quite finished lecturing me, I am going back down to the party."

Poppy stared after her in amazement. Livi always did what Poppy suggested. She'd been doing it for years. What had got into her?

It was as Poppy crossed the landing to go downstairs that she noticed that the door of her father's dark room was slightly ajar. Sitting inside in the dark, with his head in his hands, was her father.

"Dad?" she said softly. "Aren't you coming down to the party?"

"Of course, sweetheart," said her father quickly. "Just taking a breather." He stood up and to Poppy's horror a single tear glistened on his cheek. And Poppy realised that she had far more important problems to face than whether she could get Adam Reilly to ask her out.

cards on
the table

"I have to talk to you all." Mr. Field stood in the doorway of the kitchen on Sunday morning and took a deep breath.

"What about?" asked Mrs. Field, stuffing the remains of the party debris into a black plastic bag. "I really ought to be getting on with lunch."

"Will it take long?" asked Melissa. "I'm supposed to be meeting Jake at one."

Poppy felt slightly sick. This was it.

Granny Jay slipped a hand into hers. So she does know something, thought Poppy.

Leo put two hands on the kitchen table and looked at them all.

"I should have told you before," he began. "I've been a fool."

Four faces looked up at him expectantly.

CHAPTER TWENTY-EIGHT

"The business—FieldFare—it's gone," he said with a catch in his voice.

Mrs. Field gasped.

"What do you mean—gone?" she breathed.

"Just that," said Leo heavily. "The receivers come in tomorrow."

For just a moment, there was total silence in the room. The pine clock which Mrs. Field had bought on her last foray to Heals ticked relentlessly. A tap dripped rhythmically into the sink. No one moved.

Then Mrs. Field started to cry.

"No! No!" she cried, pressing her hands against her temples and shaking her head from side to side. Mr. Field took her hand. She snatched it away.

"So that's why you never paid the school fees!" shouted Melissa, jumping up from her chair and rounding on her father. "Dad, how could you do this to us?"

"It's not Dad's fault!" shouted Poppy, who wasn't really sure whose fault it was but who didn't think she could bear the pain on her father's face.

"My dear Leo, I am so very sorry," said

187

Granny Jay gently. "What's to be done?"

Poppy's father took a deep breath.

"We have to sell the house," he said. Everyone gasped in unison.

"No," whispered Mrs. Field, shaking her head in disbelief. "No. No. NO!" Her voice rose to a crescendo and then she screamed again. "No!" and jumped out of her chair and started pummelling her husband's chest with her fists. "I won't leave this house, not for you, not for anyone! I won't!"

"Celia—sit down, and shut up!" Granny Jay rose to her full four feet eleven inches, grabbed her daughter's arm and frog-marched her back to her chair. "Let Leo speak and stop the histrionics!"

Mrs. Field stopped.

"It's all my fault," admitted Poppy's father. "I was foolish enough to give the house as security on money I borrowed from the bank. I can't pay the money back and the bank has foreclosed. The Hollies has to go. And the Jag," he took a deep breath. "I lied to you—there was no accident. It was repossessed and I was too ashamed to admit it."

Granny Jay touched his hand gently.

"And Melly," he added, turning to his elder daughter, "I'm afraid we can't afford that round-the-world ticket."

Melissa's eyes widened.

"But you promised," she gasped. "All my friends know—last night—the cake—I've got the rucksack. You have to let me go."

Leo sighed. "I'm so sorry, sweetheart, but it can't be done."

Melissa stared at him, the colour draining from her face. Then she began to cry.

"I hate you!" she shouted at her father. "You've ruined everything. I shall look such a jerk in front of everyone. How could you do this to me? What will people think of us? I HATE YOU!"

"Melly!" gasped Poppy. "Don't!"

But Melissa ignored her sister and stormed out of the kitchen. Seconds later they heard her bedroom door slam.

"My house," murmured Mrs. Field, her shoulders heaving. "My beautiful, beautiful house." She stared at Leo. "And what will they say at the club?" She paused. "We can still afford the club, can't we?"

Leo shrugged.

"That," said Granny Jay tersely, "is the least of your worries. Trumped-up lot." Granny Jay had little time for the leisured classes.

"And what about Ma?" continued Mrs. Field, glaring accusingly at Leo. "You promised we could do that conversion."

Mr. Field shook his head.

"No, Celia love," he said, "*you* promised. I'm sorry, Ma," he added apologetically.

Granny Jay dismissed him with a wave of the hand.

"Worse things happen at sea," she said philosophically. "I was never sure I liked the idea anyway."

Poppy sat staring out of the window. It was like a bad dream and she kept hoping that she would suddenly wake up and find that everything was as it had always been.

"What's going to happen to us?" wailed her mother, rubbing her eyes and spreading mascara over her tear-stained cheeks. "Where will we live? What will we do?"

"We'll think of something," said Poppy's father. "Trust me."

"TRUST you? Trust you?" screamed Celia. "Look where trusting you got us. I shall never, ever trust you again!"

She jumped up from the table, knocking over her chair.

"And why did you let me spend all that money on Melissa's party if you knew this was going to happen?" she yelled.

Poppy's father sighed.

"Five hundred pounds here or there would have made little difference," he said wearily. "Just makes the overdraft a bit bigger, that's all."

"How could you be so stupid?" Poppy's mother screamed at him before running out of the room.

Mr. Field buried his head in his hands. Poppy went on staring out of the window and feeling rather sick. Granny Jay put the kettle on.

"Melly? Can I come in?" Poppy knocked tentatively on her sister's bedroom door. All she could hear was the sound of muffled sobbing.

She pushed open the door. Melissa was lying on her stomach on the bed, her shoulders shaking. Poppy sat down and put an arm on her shoulder.

"It'll be all right, Melly," she began. "Something will turn up."

Her sister rolled over onto her back and stared at Poppy.

"Oh yes, like what?" she said.

Poppy said nothing. Somehow, her words had sounded hollow, even to her. She was so used to saying things like that to her friends when they felt down, and she had never stopped to think that sometimes they didn't really help.

"You see? It's hopeless. Everything's ruined, everything! Everyone will know what's happened, we shall be a laughingstock, our friends will despise us . . ."

"No they won't," protested Poppy. "They'll be sorry for us."

"Oh great, so now we're going to be objects of pity in the neighbourhood, are we? I can't bear it!"

Poppy wanted to say that she was finding it hard to bear too. She felt like howling but she knew that wouldn't achieve anything. From downstairs she could hear her mother shouting at her dad and it seemed as if everything was falling apart. She felt very scared and rather alone.

"Melly?" she began. But before she could say more, there was a knock on the door, and Jake poked his head round.

"Can I come in?" he said.

"No!" snapped Melissa.

Jake ignored her, walked over to the bed and put an arm round her.

"It's OK, darling," he said gently, "your grand-mother told me everything. It's not the end of the world."

"Yes, it is," sobbed Melissa.

"So you have to move house," said Jake soothingly. "It's no big deal."

"Well, you wouldn't think so, would you—seeing as how you live in a grotty semi with a father who clears people's drains and a mother . . ."

"Melly!" gasped Poppy.

"Oh, go away and leave me alone!" sobbed her sister. "Both of you. Just GO!"

Poppy went. Jake followed.

the slough of despond

The next few days were awful. It was as if a huge black cloud was hanging over the household. Some days, Poppy's mother didn't bother to get dressed but spent the day wandering around in her dressing-gown, biting her normally immaculate fingernails and crying. On other days, Poppy would get home from school to find her mother made up in all the wrong colours, drinking large glasses of red wine, and talking loudly on the telephone to one of her friends. It was when Poppy heard her say things like "Wretched man" and "I shall never, ever forgive him" that she wanted to run upstairs with her hands over her ears.

Her father spent hours hunched over his calculator, punching in figures and drawing up cash flow plans, and had numerous meetings with the bank manager, from which he returned withdrawn and silent. Even the arrival of a letter from *The Sunday Times*, informing him that his entry for *Faces of Our Age* had been shortlisted for an award, failed to lift the pall of gloom surrounding him. He picked at his food and swallowed large quantities of Pepto Bismol because he kept getting a stomachache. Poppy told him to go to the doctor but he took no notice.

Melly ignored all of Jake's telephone calls, and Poppy got rather tired of having to make excuses about her being in the bath, or revising for exams, particularly since she knew that Jake didn't believe a word of it. When Nathan rang, however, Melissa was as sweet as pie, chatting in an overbright and brittle manner about the forthcoming ball and seeming not to have a care in the world.

"I'm glad Nathan's cheering you up," said Poppy, after a particularly lengthy phone call. "Why won't you talk to Jake?"

Melly's blue eyes narrowed.

"Since our dear father has scuppered our chances of ever having any money, I might as well cultivate what sources I can, mightn't I?" she snapped. "Nathan's loaded and Jake's broke—no contest."

"But Jake's much nicer than Nathan," protested Poppy. "Money isn't everything. What did Nathan say about the business going wrong?"

"I haven't told him," admitted her sister.

"But you have to!" protested Poppy.

"Not yet," said Melly. "He's taking me to The Pea Green Boat tonight and nothing's going to spoil it."

"Wow!" said Poppy. The Pea Green Boat was a floating disco restaurant moored at Kettleborough Lock and the hip place for the county set. It was also *very* expensive.

"You won't be able to keep it a secret forever," warned Poppy. "Why don't you just tell him and have done with it? It won't make any difference."

Melissa glared at her.

"What do you know? You're still a kid," she said and stomped back into her bedroom.

Poppy stared miserably after her. Everyone seemed to be changing and she didn't like it one bit.

Poppy went through the week feeling hollow. And numb. She knew the facts: they were having to sell the house, Dad had no money left, and everything would have to change. But she couldn't actually *feel* anything. And she found that the most frightening part of all.

If it hadn't been for Granny Jay, who late on Sunday afternoon had marched back to her cottage and returned with a suitcase, announcing that it was no use crying over spilt milk and she would stay until they could see the wood for the trees, Poppy didn't know how they would have managed.

It was Granny Jay who insisted that they ate regular meals, even when they protested that they were not in the slightest bit hungry. "All grief with bread is less," she would pronounce, spooning ladlefuls of chicken casserole onto their plates. It was Granny Jay who organised Poppy's mother into searching the job pages of the local paper and ignored her protests that she had never worked. It was Granny Jay who packed Leo off for long walks with his camera because she said he needed the fresh air and solitude, and made him have a round of golf, giving him a twenty pound note when he protested about wasting money. And it was Granny Jay who sorted out Poppy's big problem.

"Melly doesn't want me to say anything to anyone," she said one morning before she left for school. "But I want to tell my friends." She paused and looked at her grandmother. "I need to," she whispered.

"Of course you do," said her grandmother briskly. "A trouble shared is a trouble halved, and besides, they would be mighty put out if they thought you were unhappy and didn't trust them enough to tell them."

Poppy's eyes widened.

"I hadn't thought of it like that," she said.

Poppy was heading for the locker room when Livi caught up with her and took a long look at her solemn expression.

"What's wrong?" she asked, touching her arm.

Poppy began to tell her, and slowly the numb, dead feeling was replaced with an ache deep inside her. Tears trickled down her face.

"Oh, Poppy," said Livi, "I really am sorry. I know how you feel."

Poppy rubbed her eyes and looked at her.

"You do?"

Livi nodded.

"When we had to move because my dad kept losing jobs, I felt so empty inside, like nothing was ever going to be the same again. And then when Dad went off with Rosalie, it was like it was all starting over. So I do understand," she said.

"It's not just the money and the house and everything," sniffed Poppy. "Mum's falling apart and yelling at Dad, Melly's gone all peculiar, and I can't talk about it much because they all go into a decline."

"You can always talk to me," offered Livi.

"Thanks," said Poppy. "I thought maybe you'd gone off me."

"Whatever gave you that idea?" expostulated Livi.

"Oh you know, the Adam thing—and Luke and stuff," said Poppy.

Livi looked at her.

"Are you really keen on Adam?" she asked.

Poppy sighed.

"He's cute and sexy but right now, I can't be bothered," she said. "It all seems rather unimportant."

Livi looked rather relieved.

"Oh, and another thing," added Poppy, "Melissa doesn't want anyone to know about it, so you won't say anything, will you?"

Livi looked doubtful. "Of course not, if that's what you want," she said. "But people will have to know sometime, won't they?"

"Not just yet," insisted Poppy.

As it turned out, they all knew a lot more quickly than that.

a public announcement

"So how was the high life?" Poppy asked Melissa the following morning when she went into her bedroom.

Melissa was staring sullenly into the mirror and shrugged.

"OK, I suppose," she said flatly.

"Only OK? You get taken to *the* hot spot in the whole county by a guy who adores you and it's only OK?" Poppy eyed her sister thoughtfully. "So what went wrong?"

Melissa jumped up from her dressing table and rounded on Poppy.

"Who said anything went wrong?" she shouted. "Now just get out of my room, can't you? Leave me alone!"

A few days later, when Poppy and Melissa got

home from school, they found their parents sitting at the kitchen table looking grim-faced.

"What's the matter?" gasped Poppy. Surely something else couldn't have gone wrong?

Her mother said nothing, but thrust a copy of the *Leehampton Echo* across the table and stabbed a finger at a small column.

LOCAL BUSINESS GOES TO THE WALL

The receivers were called into FieldFare, the garden accessories company, this week as debts exceeding £150,000 were disclosed. In a written statement, FieldFare's founder director, Mr. Leo Field, expressed his sorrow at the collapse of the firm, which he blamed on the aftermath of the recession and a switch away from formalised gardens.

"Now everyone in the entire world will know!" cried Melly.

Poppy's father looked miserable.

"I'm sorry, love . . ." he began.

"Sorry? Sorry? Is that all you can say? My whole social life is in ruins and all you can say is sorry!"

She flounced out of the room, slamming the door behind her. Poppy didn't think she had ever seen her father look so hurt.

To Poppy's surprise, no one at school said a word about the piece in the paper.

"Well, I don't suppose they've seen it," said Livi, when Poppy expressed her astonishment. "I mean, the *Leehampton Echo* is hardly *The Times*, is it? The sports pages and the horoscopes are the only bits most kids read anyway."

Poppy hoped she was right.

The following evening, the telephone rang. It was Melly's friend, Vicki. Poppy yelled up the stairs and heard her sister pick up the bedroom extension.

Poppy returned to her French homework, and wondered yet again why everyone couldn't speak English and have done with it.

She was wondering what *au fond de* meant, when she heard her sister's door bang.

"Melly," she called taking the stairs two at a time, "What does *au fond . . .* What's wrong?"

Melissa was sitting at her dressing table with tears streaming down her face.

"Vicki just saw Nathan," she sobbed.

"So?" said Poppy.

"He was with Shelby Balfour," she whispered. "And they were . . ."

She sobbed louder.

"Were what?" asked Poppy anxiously.

"Kissing," wept Melissa.

Poppy gasped.

"Oh, Melly, I'm sorry," she said and stopped because it sounded fairly inadequate. How could Nathan be so insensitive, and at a time like this? And then she remembered that he didn't know anything about their problems. All the same . . .

Poppy banged her fist on the bookcase.

"How dare he treat you like that! And with Shelby Balfour—she's a real airhead if ever I knew one."

Melissa sobbed louder.

"Perhaps Vicki got it wrong," said Poppy in a desperate attempt to cheer her sister. "I mean, perhaps it was just an innocent peck on the cheek."

Melly sniffed.

"From what Vicki said, there was nothing remotely innocent about it!" she cried. "Shelby's fancied him for months and the other night, at the Pea Green Boat . . ." she hesitated.

"Yes?" said Poppy encouragingly.

"Well, I was feeling awful—you know, about Dad and everything. Everyone was making jokes and having a laugh and I just wanted to be on my own. I went up on the deck and when I came back, Shelby was dancing really close with Nathan and flirting something rotten."

"Tart!" muttered Poppy.

"And then Nathan said to me that he thought Shelby was really cool and why couldn't I loosen up and be more of a raver like her. And now I've lost him—I know I have!"

Melissa burst into a fresh bout of weeping.

"Don't cry, Melly," Poppy said. "He's not worth it. He didn't even have the decency to tell you to your face. Forget him."

"But I love him!" cried Melly.

Poppy wasn't sure that this protesting of devotion was strictly true but thought it kinder not to say anything.

"You've still got Jake," Poppy reminded her.

"Jake and me are finished," snapped Melissa.

"Supper's ready!" called Granny Jay from the

bottom of the stairs.

"Are you coming?" queried Poppy.

Melissa shook her head.

"I shall never eat again," she wailed. "My life is as good as over."

"Now then," said Granny Jay firmly as the rest of the family sat down to sausage pie, "this has all got to stop."

"What has?" asked Mrs. Field halfheartedly.

"All this moping around," said Granny Jay. "Now Leo, when is this house going up for sale?"

"Next week," said Mr. Field.

So soon, thought Poppy. She had kept hoping for a miracle, but it seemed miracles were in short supply.

"So where will you live?" demanded Granny Jay.

"That," said Leo, "is the six-million-dollar question. Somewhere cheap, that's for sure."

"One of those flats in the town centre?" suggested Granny Jay. "It would be nice to have you nearby."

Poppy suddenly had a flash of inspiration.

"I think I have the solution," she announced.

207 ✳

Three pairs of eyes raised expectantly.

"Charley's moving out, right Gran?" Her grandmother nodded, a spark of recognition gleaming in her eye.

"So we rent Charley's cottage," announced Poppy.

"Charley's cottage?" Poppy's mother spat out the words. "That rundown dump?"

Granny Jay bristled.

"Charley's cottage is not a dump, any more than mine is," she said. "It's a brilliant plan, Poppy darling. And just think—we'd be neighbours. I could help you out . . ."

"And we could still keep an eye on you," declared Poppy.

"That," said her grandmother, "is beside the point."

"It just might be the solution," said Poppy's father thoughtfully.

Poppy's mother slammed her fist on the table.

"Do you think I want to end up where I started, in some poky little cottage by a slime infested canal? You may be content to live there but I'm not. We've made a name for ourselves round here, you know," she added.

"Names don't pay bills," commented Granny Jay acerbically.

"And those cottages do have a lot of character," said Mr. Field tactfully.

Granny Jay looked slightly appeased.

"Well now," she said, "you'll be wanting to think it all through, and I've got this book to finish, so I'll be off upstairs to my room." She gathered up her belongings and turned to face her daughter.

"And remember, Celia," she said quietly, "there's nothing so bad but it might have been worse. Ill luck is always good for something."

"Oh be quiet, Ma!" retorted Poppy's mother.

Granny Jay inclined her head but said nothing.

"Good night, Gran," said Poppy.

"Night, night, sweetheart," replied her grandmother, climbing the stairs. "You are a clever girl. Night, Melly angel," she called through Melissa's closed bedroom door.

She got no reply.

* * *

"We might be moving to Canal End," said Poppy to Melissa when she went to give her some cold pie and salad, "to Charley's cottage, next door to Gran."

Melissa turned dull eyes towards her.

"Oh yes?"

Poppy waited for the explosion, the remarks about how demeaning it would be to live at the wrong end of town and protests about the damage it would do to her social standing.

But Melly said nothing. She just stared at the ceiling.

Poppy would have preferred an outburst.

poppy's mother rallies

Poppy wished that Melly hadn't stopped seeing Jake. She was finding her French homework impossible and he would have sped through it in next to no time.

Her mother came into the kitchen just as she was adding a few accents on assorted letters to make it look as if she knew what she was doing.

"Like some hot chocolate, Poppy?"

Poppy was so delighted to see her mother doing something again that she would have gladly eaten a three-course meal to please her.

"I've been thinking about jobs," said Mrs. Field measuring milk into the pan. "Granny Jay's right—what's done is done, and I shall have to do something—the trouble is, I don't have any skills."

Poppy jumped up and hugged her mother.

"That's nonsense!" she cried. "You're brilliant at all sorts of things."

"Like what?" asked her mother wryly.

"Playing tennis," began Poppy.

"Hardly in the Steffi Graf league," said her mother.

"You can cook like a dream," continued Poppy.

Her mother pursed her lips.

"That's a thought," she said. "Poppy, be an angel and take a mug of chocolate up to Gran before she falls asleep. I just want to look something up."

poppy's world turns upside down

"It's chocolate time!" chirped Poppy brightly, knocking on the spare bedroom door.

There was no reply. Once Granny Jay got absorbed in a book, she was in a world of her own.

Poppy pushed open the door and walked in, slopping chocolate on the carpet and hastily rubbing it in with her foot.

Her grandmother appeared to have nodded off over her P. D. James.

"Wake up, Gran—Mum's made you some chocolate."

Granny Jay didn't move.

Poppy moved nearer the bed.

"Gran?" she whispered.

CHAPTER THIRTY-TWO

Her grandmother's eyes were open but totally blank and a tiny rivulet of saliva was trickling down her chin.

Poppy stared at her.

"Gran? Gran! Gran!" she shouted louder.

In the pit of her stomach was a great stone weight and her mouth was so dry that her tongue seemed to stick to the roof of it.

And then she screamed.

Granny Jay was dead. Granny Jay was dead. Poppy lay in bed repeating the words in her head and yet she still couldn't believe it was true.

She wanted to cry but she couldn't. She hadn't been able to ever since the moment when the paramedic raised his eyes from Granny Jay's prone body and slowly shook his head. She had made countless cups of tea, comforted her sobbing mother and weeping sister, and told her father that of course it wasn't his fault, and that Granny Jay's death had nothing to do with his bad news.

"I feel so awful!" her mother had wept after they had taken Granny Jay away. "The very last words I said to her were 'Be quiet!'. How could I have been so heartless? She was only trying to help and now she's gone!"

"I didn't even say goodnight to her," wept Melissa. "She called out to me and I didn't answer."

Poppy didn't know what to say to either of them so she made some more tea and wondered why she felt as if she was acting a part in a play. She had put off going to bed for as long as she could because she didn't want to walk past the spare bedroom with its stripped bed where only hours before Granny Jay had been lying.

And now she was in bed and she still couldn't cry and she couldn't sleep. She couldn't believe that her grandmother was never again going to sit in their kitchen putting the world to rights or penning angry letters to the local paper about the state of the pavements or the irregularity of the Canal End bus service. She would never tell Poppy her skirts were too short or tease Melly about having more boyfriends than most people had hot dinners.

Melly. Perhaps she was lying awake feeling

awful too. Poppy slipped out of bed, crossed the landing, and quietly opened the door of Melissa's bedroom.

Melissa wasn't there.

Poppy was beginning to panic. She had hunted through every room of the house but there was no sign of her sister. It was three o'clock in the morning. Where could she be?

She went through to the kitchen and just before she switched on the light, she caught sight of someone sitting on the bench at the bottom of the garden. For a moment she was terrified, and then as her eyes grew accustomed to the dark, she realised it was her sister.

She opened the back door and went out.

"Melly?" she said. "Melly, what are you doing out here?"

Her sister gave her a blank stare and said nothing.

"Melly, you'll freeze to death—come on inside."

Still saying nothing, Melissa allowed Poppy to lead her indoors.

"What is it, Melly? What's the matter?" said Poppy.

"It's all so pointless," said her sister in a flat voice. "Nothing lasts, does it? Nothing at all."

"You mean Granny Jay?" said Poppy choking back tears. "She was old, you know."

Melly shook her head. Her hair was tousled and she had smudges of mascara on her cheeks.

"Not just that," she said. "I loved Nathan and he's gone. Jake was a good mate and I drove him away. We had a lovely home and now we've lost that. It's as if anything that ever matters gets taken away from you. So what's the point?"

Poppy took her sister's hand.

"It seems like that now, I know," she said. "But you deserve better than Nathan, and Jake hasn't gone—he'd come back like a shot if you asked him."

Melly shook her head disconsolately.

"And we'll have another home and you'll go off to uni and make loads of new friends and have men falling at your feet in the throes of unmitigated passion," she said, trying to make Melly laugh.

"I won't get to uni," said Melissa.

"Don't be daft, Cambridge already said they want you," retorted Poppy.

Melly looked at her, and the blank expression melted into tears.

"I can't work anymore, Poppy," she whispered. "My brain won't function; I can't remember anything I ever learned." She wiped a hand across her face.

"I'm going to fail my A-levels, Poppy," she sobbed. "I know I am."

poppy to the rescue

The next day neither Poppy nor Melissa went to school. Poppy's father spent hours on the telephone telling friends and relatives about Granny Jay's death and making arrangements for the funeral. He was taking charge and seemed more dynamic and in control than he had for weeks.

Poppy had a huge lump in her throat and a pain in her chest. She thought people were supposed to sob and howl when someone they loved died, but she couldn't. She even tried to, but the tears wouldn't come. It was as if everything was on hold, like a picture on a video after you've pressed the Pause button.

Poppy's mother was trying to be very brave, and insisted on cooking them all a three-course lunch because that was what Granny Jay would have done if she had still been with them. She spent hours polishing the furniture and tidying the magazine racks and when Poppy told her dad that she thought Mum should rest, he simply said that everyone had to find their own way of coping and they should let her be.

But it wasn't her mother that was causing Poppy the most anxiety. That morning, when she had sneaked into Melissa's room to check she was finally catching up on some sleep, she had noticed that all her exam notes were stuffed in her wastepaper basket. The letter from Cambridge University offering her a place, which had been pinned in pride of place on her cork noticeboard, had been scrawled over with black marker pen and SOME HOPE written in big letters.

But what worried Poppy most was that on Melly's bedside table was a bottle of the little green pills that her mum took to try to dampen down her fear of flying. That was when Poppy made her decision.

"It's Melly—our gran died and now she's saying everything's hopeless and I saw these pills beside her bed and—please, please," pleaded Poppy down the phone. "You are the only person who can sort it out. She needs you, Jake. You will come, won't you?"

"I'm on my way," said Jake. And Poppy was glad that he had never been someone to waste time on words.

Poppy was never quite sure what Jake said or what he did. He had turned up in his daisy-painted van, and presented Poppy's mother with a bunch of daffodils.

"It's hard to know what to say to you, Mrs. Field," he said. "But I want you to know that if there's anything I can do I will."

Poppy's mother gave him a spontaneous hug. He seemed rather pleased.

Then he disappeared upstairs.

Melly and Jake had gone out for a walk. Melly was still looking blank-faced but she was dressed and Poppy noticed with satisfaction that when Jake slipped his hand into hers, she did not protest. As she watched them together, Poppy wished there was someone around to take charge of her.

Poppy was sitting on her bed looking at old photos of Granny Jay when there was a knock on the door.

"Can I come in?"

It was Livi.

She didn't say anything. She just sat beside Poppy and hugged her. And slowly, Poppy began to cry. And cry. And cry.

And still Livi sat there.

"I'm sorry," sniffed Poppy. "Now I've started I can't stop."

"There's nothing to be sorry for," said Livi. "You're my friend."

more bad news for poppy

Everyone was very nice to Poppy when she went back to school. Hayley gave her a little white bear with the message "Consider Yourself Hugged" and Tamsin bought her a scented candle that was supposed to make you feel energetic. But whenever she started talking about Granny Jay, they changed the subject. It was as if they thought that by not mentioning her name, Poppy would forget and be happy. So she smiled and joined in all their jokes and sometimes she managed to go for several hours without the hollow feeling in her stomach. But it always came back.

At home, everyone was trying to put on a very brave face. Granny Jay's funeral had been held at the church she had attended all her life, and although the sight of the walnut coffin with its two wreaths—one from the family and one from Charley—made Poppy's eyes fill with tears, she was sure Granny Jay would have been proud to see the church so full of people. They all said very nice things about her grandmother, calling her "a real diamond" and saying that when they made her they broke the mould. There was a lot of hymn singing, because Granny Jay had written in her will that she didn't want a lot of misery and all in all, Poppy felt it was more of a joyful celebration of her life than a miserable marking of her death.

Melissa was seeing Jake again and Poppy was relieved when one evening she found her sister writing an economics essay.

"Are you feeling better now?" she asked.

Melly nodded.

"I'm still worried about getting to uni," she confessed. "Everyone thinks I am so clever— what if I fluff?"

"If you fluff, you try again, or do something different," said Poppy.

Melly laughed.

"You really do have life sussed, don't you?" she said.

"Not really," said Poppy. And realised she didn't.

Melissa ruled a line and closed her book.

"And guess what?" she said. "I'm still going to take my Gap year and get a job for six months and then go to Spain and work in a beach bar for the summer with Jake."

Poppy grinned.

"So it's really on with Jake?"

Melly nodded.

"I was mad at you at first for getting in touch with him," she confessed. "But that was because I knew I had been mean to him, and I hated myself. He said it didn't matter," she added.

"That," said Poppy, "is because he's mad about you."

Melissa smiled.

"Melly, those tablets by your bed . . ." ventured Poppy.

Melly sighed.

"I know, I know, it was stupid," she confessed.

"I only took three. I just wanted to sleep and sleep and forget about everything—and then, as soon as I had swallowed three I got worried and stopped."

"Well, it was very silly," snapped Poppy.

"I know," replied her sister. "And you are right, Poppy," she added.

"What about?" said Poppy.

"Jake does have a nice body."

Melissa laughed. It was the nicest sound Poppy had heard for two weeks.

Perhaps now everyone could put their problems behind them once and for all. But Poppy had one more hurdle to cross before that could happen.

"Poppy, have you finished your homework?" It was Monday evening and Poppy was desperately trying to catch up with the work she had missed.

"More or less," said Poppy. "I hate electromagnetics."

She expected her father to make some quip, but he just sank into a chair and looked at her.

"I've had a few discussions with the bursar," he

began, fiddling with the end of his tie. "I would have told you sooner, but what with Granny Jay and everything . . ." his voice tapered off.

"Told me what?" asked Poppy.

"I am afraid you are going to have to leave Bellborough Court."

Poppy stared open-mouthed at her father. Not that. Not on top of everything else. Please not that, she thought.

"You see, they're going to let Melly stay till the end of the summer term because of her A levels," he explained. "But I am two and a half terms behind with the fees and they just won't keep you on for free. I am so sorry, darling."

Poppy swallowed. She couldn't bear the thought of leaving Bellborough.

"I've spoken to Mr. Todd at Lee Hill, and he'll be delighted to have you," said her father encouragingly. "It's high up in the league tables, and it's not as if you've started your GCSE work yet. You'll be fine there."

Oh yes, thought Poppy miserably. Poppy will be fine. Poppy is the strong one, the sensible one. She won't care.

But she didn't feel fine and she did care. She cared heaps. Maybe Melly had been right—everything you valued did disappear. She felt tears welling up and she bit her lip so hard it hurt.

"Poppy, say something," said her father.

But Poppy didn't want to talk. She didn't want to listen. She just wanted to be alone.

She shook her head and pushed past her father. Mumbling that she was going for some fresh air, she ran out into the garden and through the back gate. She didn't know where she was going and she didn't really care.

charley
offers some
consolation

Poppy walked and walked and found herself standing on the bridge over the canal staring across at Granny Jay's cottage. There was a bottle of milk on the step. Milk that Granny Jay would never drink, thought Poppy miserably.

Through the blur of her tears, she saw someone peering into the sitting room window. It was Charley Rust.

She wiped her eyes and walked slowly over the bridge and along the canal side path.

"Hello, Charley," she said softly.

"Well, me duck, me lovely," he said, taking her arm. "And how are you? When your dad came and told me about Beryl, I . . ." He stopped and blew his nose on a huge red handkerchief.

Poppy bit her lip.

"I still can't believe it," she admitted. "I keep thinking she'll open the door and ask me in for a cup of tea and tell me my skirt is too short."

Charley smiled.

"Always spoke her mind, did Beryl," he said. He stared out over the canal for a moment and then turned to Poppy.

"Well now," he said. "You had better come in and have a cup of tea."

He took Poppy's hand and led her into his cottage. Blisworth the cat forsook his normally standoffish manner and rubbed himself against her legs. Around the room were piles of cardboard boxes filled with ornaments and pictures. Charley took an elderly kettle off the stove and filled it with water.

"I shan't mind so much now," said Charley at last.

"Pardon?" said Poppy.

"Going," said Charley. "They're coming for me tomorrow—Jennifer and that stuck-up husband of hers. Going to move me into the home. I was dreading it—but then, with Beryl gone the place doesn't seem the same." He gazed out of the window as a brightly painted narrow-boat chugged by.

"You were good mates, weren't you?" said Poppy.

Charley broke into a grin and nudged her.

"More than mates, your gran and me," he said with a wheezy chuckle. "Much more than just mates."

Poppy's eyes widened.

"Charley!" she gasped. "You don't mean . . ."

Charley nodded. He shuffled to the sideboard, opened a drawer, and handed Poppy a photo-graph in a cardboard folder. It showed Charley and Granny Jay, arms round each other's waist, licking cotton candy on some seaside promenade.

Poppy's eyes widened.

"But, I mean, you're old . . ." she began.

"Not always we weren't," said Charley indig-nantly. "And besides, there's many a good tune played on an old fiddle, as your gran would have said!"

"I am going to miss her so much," said Poppy. "Everything is going wrong all at once."

"Everything?" questioned Charley, pulling up a saggy armchair and gesturing to Poppy to sit down.

And Poppy found herself telling him all about having to move house, and Dad not having any money, and how miserable they all were.

"And now," she sniffed, "Dad says I've got to leave Bellborough and go to Lee Hill. And I don't want to."

Charley took her hand in his weather-beaten one, squeezed it, and looked her straight in the eye.

"Well, that could be wonderful," he said.

"*Wonderful?*" exclaimed Poppy. "How can you say that? Haven't you been listening to a word I've been saying?"

Charley nodded calmly.

"Oh yes, me duck, I've been listening," he assured her. "Remember what you told me when I said I didn't want to move house? You said that I should be looking forward to this new phase— making plans, getting excited."

"I did, didn't I," agreed Poppy thoughtfully. "It all seemed so easy when it was your problem. But leaving all my friends . . ."

"The real friends will still be around—and the ones that drift away weren't worth having in the first place," said Charley firmly.

"I just wish it wasn't all happening so fast," said Poppy.

Charley sucked on his teeth.

"Seems to me that once you know you have to do something, it's best to get on with it. No good hanging on to something that's gone—like me and this here cottage," he said.

"And remember what your Gran used to say? 'God never shuts a door . . .'"

"'Without opening a window,'" finished Poppy. "Oh Charley, I am going to miss her."

"Me too," said Charley. They sat for a moment or two in companionable silence.

Then Charley leaned forward and patted her knee.

"That book," he said, "we'll write about her in it, shall we? A kind of memorial in words—to hand down to posterity."

233 ✳

Poppy considered.

"I like that idea," she said. "I like that very much. As soon as you're settled in Victoria House, we'll start. I'll get a loose-leaf book and we'll do a bit each weekend. We'll need to start with when you were a little boy and go on from there and then . . ."

"That's it," said Charley, smiling at her new-found eagerness, "always look to the future."

"Yes," said Poppy. "I'll try."

a new side to luke

The next afternoon, Poppy had a free period. She was sitting on the games pavilion steps trying to read *Sense and Sensibility*.

But all she could think about was Granny Jay. She thought she should be over it all by now, but she couldn't help thinking about how she would never be able to discuss her problems with her, and wondering what she would have said about Poppy going to Lee Hill. She knew that Charley was right, and that it was pointless to try to ignore changes when they happened, but suddenly she couldn't help feeling that everyone else's life was a total doddle compared to hers.

"It hurts like hell, doesn't it?"

Poppy turned to see Luke squatting down beside her.

"I know how you feel," he said, not waiting for her to reply.

"Do you?" said Poppy, and then kicked herself for not remembering about his mum.

Luke nodded.

"After my mum died, everyone tried to jolly me along. Oh, they meant well, I know that now, but at the time it was like they weren't even acknowledging that Mum had ever lived. They seemed to think that by talking about other things and taking me out for the day the pain would somehow disappear. It doesn't."

"No," agreed Poppy, "it doesn't."

"It will get better," said Luke. "But don't listen to anyone who tells you not to talk about it. Talk about it all you like—it's the only way to get through it."

Poppy tried not to cry.

"You can cry," said Luke in a matter-of-fact manner. "Better out than in, that's what Mum used to say."

Poppy giggled despite herself.

"So did my gran," she said. And she found herself telling Luke all about the funny things

Gran used to say and how she always wore knitted hats in hideous colours and how she bossed everyone about.

"Like you?" smiled Luke. And Poppy realised he wasn't taking the Mickey, just saying he understood.

And once Poppy had started, she couldn't stop. She told Luke about the business collapsing and the house having to be sold and how wretched she felt.

"And the worst bit is, I have to leave Bellborough."

Luke looked aghast.

"Where are you going?" he asked.

"Lee Hill," said Poppy.

"Oh good, not far away," he said. And dropped his eyes.

"I wouldn't like it if you went miles away," he added. "Look, will you come out on Saturday? Nothing heavy—we could go for a walk and talk about your gran if you like."

Poppy looked at him thoughtfully.

"That's really nice of you," she said. "I'd like that."

Luke grinned and Poppy considered that he was, after all, really quite good-looking.

Come to think of it, thought Poppy, Luke Cunningham was a very warm and understanding person. She began to wonder whether, after all, she had been wrong in ever thinking that Livi was quite right for him.

moving issues

Poppy felt strangely lighthearted. Talking to Luke made her realise that she wasn't the first person to feel hurt and confused and it didn't matter that for once, she didn't have all the answers. She began to think that, after all, she might come through all this.

When she and Melly got home that afternoon, they found their parents sitting over a cup of tea looking surprisingly happy.

"Hello, darling," said Mrs. Field. "I've got some news."

She told Poppy that Granny Jay had left them her cottage in her will.

"So we can move in, and then at least we won't have to worry about rent," she said.

Melissa looked up in surprise.

"But it's so small!" she protested. "It will be

a frightful squash, and besides, I thought you said that the last thing you wanted to do was move back there."

Mrs. Field nodded.

"I did," she admitted. "But when I started to think about things, I realised that all that really matters is that we pull through this together. And somehow, it will be like being closer to Granny Jay, having her old home. That's not to say I won't moan like crazy when the sideboard won't fit," she added smiling wryly.

She took a deep breath. "I'm still miserable and fed up—and angry half the time. But what's done is done, and now we have to sort it out. And thanks to Poppy, it won't be nearly as crowded in the cottage as you think."

"Me?" said Poppy. "What did I do?"

Mrs. Field smiled.

"You suggested renting Charley's cottage," she said. "I went to see him today and he is tickled pink by the idea. So with the two cottages, we'll have plenty of space."

She grinned at Poppy.

"I thought you could have Charley's bedroom

and spare room as your own mini flatlet," she said.

"Neat," exclaimed Poppy. "Can I have new wallpaper? Or is that too expensive?" she added, remembering their cash problems.

"I think," said her father, "we might just be able to manage that."

The next two weeks flew past. Once she had told Luke about leaving school, she found it easier to tell everyone else. Livi was distraught.

"I shall miss you so badly," she said. "You're my best friend."

Poppy grinned.

"I won't be far away," she said. "You can still come round. We're moving to Gran's cottage and renting the one next door and I am getting to have two rooms all to myself."

"Cool!" said Livi. "Can I come and stay?"

"Of course," said Poppy.

She was beginning to feel better.

Poppy and Luke went for a long walk along the canal. He told her about his mum and she talked about Granny Jay and Charley and they discovered they both loathed reggae, loved costume dramas, and totally failed to understand chemistry. When Poppy told Luke she wanted to be an agony aunt and have her own show, he didn't laugh but simply said he thought she would be very good at it, and confessed that he wanted to be a professional musician and play in a famous symphony orchestra.

Just before they parted company at the top of Ecton Lane, Luke kissed her lightly on the cheek. Then he kissed her again. On the lips. For quite a long time. Poppy found she didn't mind him kissing. Not at all.

When she got home, she found her mother in tour guide mode, showing a family round their house.

"And this is our rather splendid sitting room," she enthused. "The fireplace is Italian marble, you know."

Poppy stuck her head round the door.

"And this is Poppy, my daughter," said Mrs. Field.

"I'm not for sale," remarked Poppy and everyone laughed.

"The Banerjis are thinking of buying the house," said Mrs. Field. "Their children go to Lee Hill."

Poppy smiled tentatively at a dark-haired girl with huge eyes and a boy who was looking distinctly bored.

"I hear you will be starting there next term," said Mrs. Banerji. "You'll love it, won't she, Sumitha?"

"As much as it is possible to love any school," said Sumitha and grinned at Poppy. She had dark brown eyes and shoulder-length black hair plaited in tiny braids. She looked really friendly.

"Do you want to come upstairs and see my room?" offered Poppy. "You can give me the lowdown on what gives at Lee Hill."

Half an hour later, Poppy had discovered that Mr. Todd the headmaster was very keen on pupil participation, that the school magazine was getting mega boring and needed revitalising because Laura Turnbull, who used to do it, was writing a history of the school for centenary year, and that Miss McConnell was setting up a World Awareness Group to discuss important social issues of the day.

"I think," said Poppy, "I might like it at Lee Hill."

"It's a bit of a coincidence, me being here today, isn't it?" said Sumitha.

And Poppy could have sworn she heard Granny Jay's voice saying "Coincidences, my dear, are God's way of offering you an opportunity."

Poppy was feeling better all the time.

farewells

Although Poppy was dreading the last week of term, she ended up having a pretty good time.

Adam asked her out and they went Rollerblading and to the cinema. He took Livi out, too, and Tamsin, and Hayley. In fact, Adam Reilly seemed to be playing the field with great enthusiasm. Strangely enough, Poppy didn't mind. She found she enjoyed the long country walks with Luke far more, because they spent the time talking about all the things they couldn't find anyone else to listen to.

Melissa announced that Pizza Palace had offered her a job as soon as her exams were over and that she was also going to teach maths in the evenings and holidays to kids who were struggling with their courses.

"That way, I can save enough cash for me and Jake to go to Spain and maybe even

CHAPTER THIRTY-EIGHT

Tunisia and Morocco," she told the family over supper.

"Do I get free pizzas?" asked Poppy.

"No," said Melissa.

"After all I've done for you," moaned Poppy teasingly.

Two days before the end of term, the Fields moved out of the Hollies and into Canal End Cottages. Since the day coincided with double physics, Poppy offered to stay at home and help, but her mother was adamant that she should go and spend as much time as possible with her friends.

"Besides," she said, "I don't want you under my feet telling me what I mustn't throw away."

Poppy knew that her mum was putting on a brave face and her dad, who was in the garden dismantling the rotary washing line was trying to whistle "Wish Me Luck As You Wave Me Good-bye" in an attempt at jollity. Poppy wasn't fooled.

"It'll work out, Mum, you'll see," she said, squeezing her mother's hand.

"I know it will, love," said her mother. "It's just today that's going to be hard."

As Poppy walked down the drive, she turned to look back at The Hollies. She couldn't remember living anywhere else; she had only been fifteen months old when they moved there. The thought that she would never again sit at the big pine table in the kitchen, or curl up on the window seat under the eaves in her bedroom made her feel very lost.

As she turned the corner, she was surprised to see Luke waiting for her.

"What are you doing here?" she said. "Your stop is miles back."

"It's today you move, isn't it?" asked Luke.

Poppy nodded.

"I thought you might like a bit of company," he explained. "It will turn out fine, you know, even if it doesn't feel like it now."

Luke always seemed to know what to say, thought Poppy. He never handed you a load of silly platitudes and told you not to worry.

"You are so nice," said Poppy and knew she really meant it.

"So are you," said Luke. "Very."

* * *

At the end of term disco, Poppy's year presented her with a huge cartoon that Tamsin had drawn, showing Poppy as a newspaper agony aunt, almost buried in piles of letters and brandishing a big placard that read:

**POPPY SORTS
EVERYTHING!**

Mrs. Joll said PSE lessons would not be the same without Poppy's "lively contribution and lateral thinking," a remark Poppy thought would greatly enhance her cv. Everyone hugged her and wished her luck and she laughed and cried and promised to keep in touch and then someone said that Lee Hill was actually only four miles from Bellborough and why were they all talking as if Poppy were going to the North Pole, and they all laughed again.

And then, while they were dancing, Luke, who had spent the entire evening at her side, told her that he loved her.

"It's OK," he said hastily, looking flushed and confused, "I'm not expecting you to love me back."

Poppy looked up at him and took his hand.

"You might have to put up with me doing just that," she said and kissed him.

in camera

There were only three weeks between Bellborough breaking up and Lee Hill starting the summer term but they were full of activity.

Livi, Tamsin, and Hayley spent three days helping Poppy decorate the two rooms that had been Charley's bedrooms. They painted Poppy's bedroom with coloured emulsion paint and stuck an Indian frieze of little fat elephants and sleepy-looking tigers halfway up the wall, but by the time they came to do the den they got very adventurous and decided to rag roll the walls. They made a frightful mess and spent more time rolling around in hysterical giggles than actually working, and in the end Poppy's dad had to help them finish. But Mrs. Field said it was nice to hear them so happy and since it was Poppy's room she could clear up the mess.

There were bad days too. Poppy found her

mum sobbing into the potato peelings one day, because she couldn't find space for her bow-fronted china cabinet. Melissa was revising for her A levels one morning when she saw Nathan and a willowy chestnut-haired girl walking arm in arm along the towpath towards the Boatman Inn.

"He *is* gorgeous," she sighed to Poppy.

"He is a swine," said Poppy curtly. "I'll test you on your math."

Her father wrote countless job applications for posts he didn't really want, but then got most depressed when companies told him he was too old.

"Fifty-one isn't old," he kept repeating, partly to convince himself.

"Don't worry," said Poppy. "Something will turn up."

And because she was Poppy Field, she was right. It was on the last day of the school holidays that Poppy was crossing the bridge to Canal End Cottages after spending the day cycling with Luke, when she saw a cluster of people on the towpath. Two of them had notepads and one was lining up a camera on a tripod. Her father was standing on the step looking rather self-conscious and her mother was hastily applying some lipstick and patting her hair into place.

"What's going on?" said Poppy, pushing past a young girl in a flying jacket who was brandishing a pocket tape recorder.

"Darling, there you are!" her mother cried. "You'll never guess what—Dad's won!"

"Won what?" asked Poppy.

"That photographic competition—*Faces of Our Age* in *The Sunday Times*. They phoned this morning. The prize is three thousand pounds! The *Echo* are doing a piece about him and this lady is from *In Focus*."

"And it's all thanks to you," said her father, grinning rather absurdly into a camera.

"Me?" queried Poppy.

"You were the one who brought Ada home, and the picture that won was the one I took of her on the lock gate," he reminded her.

"Excuse me, Mr. Field," said the girl with the notepad. "But could you just tell me your plans for the future?"

She licked her pencil and looked expectant.

"I'm going to take up photography in a professional capacity," announced her father.

"Dad!" gasped Poppy. "Really?"

"Leo?" queried Mrs. Field.

Leo's face broke into a huge grin.

"Just look around you." He waved a hand towards the canal where several narrowboats were chugging towards moorings and a group of children were playing Pooh Sticks from one of the lock gates. "It's all there—waiting to be captured."

"Excuse me, sir," ventured a photographer. "Perhaps a shot of you with Mrs. Field and your daughter?"

They stood on the step and tried to look natural, which meant they didn't.

"You remember I said I had a few things up my sleeve?" Poppy's father continued. "Well, I've worked it all out. I've got a couple of commissions from the newspaper to take pictures of canal life, and then I'm going to do a whole series of shots for calendars. In the season I can do family shots for visitors, and the Golf Club want to make me their official photographer for tournaments."

He beamed.

"Dad, that's brilliant!" cried Poppy. "You could become another Lord Lichfield. You'll be rich and famous."

Her father laughed.

"Right now, Poppy love, I'll settle for being happy and working," he said.

new beginnings

The last few days of the holidays were pretty amazing. Mr. Field appeared on TV East and Radio Leehampton and Layla Binns-Fincham, an enormous woman with an unrestrained chest, came down from *The Sunday Times Magazine* to write what she called "a profile of the man behind the lens." The editor of a very upmarket country magazine telephoned and asked for more portraits of what she called "local eccentrics" and Poppy dragged him along to Victoria House to capture Charley for posterity while she embarked on the first chapter of *Rust on the Lock.*

They found Charley ensconced on a wooden seat in the gardens, deep in conversation with a woman in a very familiar hat from which protruded a twig full of dangling catkins.

CHAPTER FORTY

"Hi, Charley!" called Poppy. And then she saw that his guest was Ada.

"This is wonderful!" cried Mr. Field, and launched into the saga of the winning portrait and his indebtedness to Ada.

"And this," he said with a flourish, "is for you."

He handed Ada a cheque for £500.

Ada stared at it open-mouthed.

"And before you say a word," said Mr. Field, "it's from the newspaper, not me. Your reward for being the winning model. They asked for an address but I told them you were in the throes of moving."

Ada threw back her head and roared with laughter.

"Me—the Kate Moss of the road," she chortled.

Mr. Field looked a little embarrassed.

"Now look, I mean, if you don't have a bank account, I can quite easily make arrangements . . ."

"Oh, my dear sir," said Ada. "I have three accounts. I think I shall pop this into Premium Reserve—saving for a rainy day." She winked at him.

"I thought . . ." began Poppy and then stopped because what she had been thinking might be deemed rather rude.

"You thought I was a penniless old tramp with nothing to do but live off charity," said Ada with a gentle smile. "My dear, I wander about when the mood takes me, and then I toddle back to my flat for a while, and then, when the old leg muscles start twitching, I'm off again. I don't have a family, I've no one to answer to."

She patted Poppy's arm.

"And one day, my love, you will come to see that sometimes you have to do what you have to do."

"So how come you're here?" asked Poppy.

"Trespassing!" chuckled Charley. "I found her in the hedge."

"I was," said Ada, in as dignified a manner as she could muster, "merely assessing the availability of some fresh decoration for my hat." She patted the said headpiece affectionately. "One must never let oneself go, you know."

She surveyed her audience with puzzlement.

"Why are you all laughing?" she asked.

poppy
makes her
mark again

It was on her third day at Lee Hill that Poppy decided to take matters in hand. She had already joined the World Awareness discussion group, signed up for trials for the basketball team, and offered to write an article on bereavement for the school magazine. She had come to the conclusion that Miss McConnell's PSE lessons should be handled slightly differently and had made friends with Kim Saunders, who definitely needed guidance on being more assertive. She had written to three publishing houses, informing them that *Rust on the Lock* would be available by the end of August and suggesting that they might like to hold an auction at which she would sell to the highest bidder.

She was surprised that, to date, she had received no reply.

It was when Mr. Todd announced in Assembly that the school desperately needed a new editor for the school magazine, now that Laura Turnbull was taken up with what he called greater things, that Poppy had her idea. She hoped Mr. Todd would be more receptive than Gee-Gee.

Straightening her new navy skirt, which she had to admit was rather more fashionable than Bellborough's maroon pleats, she knocked on his study door.

"Enter!"

Mr. Todd beamed a welcome.

"It's Poppy Field, isn't it? Settling in well, are you?"

Poppy nodded.

"Very well, thank you, sir," she said.

"And what can I do for you, Poppy?" enquired the headmaster.

"I rather think, sir," said Poppy, "that it is more a question of what I can do for you."

259 ✳

glossary

A levels: advanced-level examinations, exams to receive high school diploma

Advert: advertisement

Agony Aunt/Uncle: advice columnist

Bin: garbage can

Bonnet: hood of the car

Brill: brilliant, wonderful

Casualty: emergency room

Chuffed: psyched, smugly pleased

Comprehensive: public school

Cred: reputation

Crisps: potato chips

Daft: stupid

Double glazing: windows

Flat: apartment

Gap year: taking a year off before going to university

GCSE's: senior exams to pass eleventh grade

Gear: clothes, belongings

Git: jerk

Gobsmacked: shocked

Go spare: freak out

Grotty: gross, dirty

Hiccup: small problem

Kit: gear

Loo: bathroom

Mac: raincoat

Mad: crazy

Made redundant: fired, laid off

Mate: friend

MP: Member of Parliament

Naff: dorky, cheesy

On the dole: unemployed

Oz: Australia

Poxy: disgusting

Prang: an accident

Prat: fool

Public school: private school

Queue: line

Revision: studying for tests and exams

Row: fight

Rubbish: garbage

Ruck: scuffle, fight

Rucksack: backpack

Semi: semi-detached house

Spanner: wrench

Suss: find, figure out

Taking the mickey: make fun of

Uni: university

Well shot of: well rid of